I

T0096256

Dr Fahd Razy graduated from ▓▓▓▓▓▓ ▓▓▓▓ in Ireland and is currently a practicing medical officer at Hospital Sultanah Nur Zahira, Kuala Terengganu. Started producing creative writing since 2000, he had been writing in various genres including short-stories, poetries, play-script, anecdotes, essays, and other non-fictional writings. Among his published books include *Menggeledah Nurani* (poetry), *Ikan dalam Jiwa* (poetry), *Kota Subuh* (poetry), *Pascasejarah* (novel), *Cinta Menyala di Constantinople* (short-stories), *Mencari Tuhan* (play-script), *Sains Menulis Puisi* (poetry guide-book), and 'Enam Tulisan Skema tentang Puisi' (essays). He also wrote medical related non-literature books including *Cakar Ayam Seorang Doktor, Doktor tanpa Kot Putih, Bukan Doktor Gugel, Rokok Terakhir di dalam Asbak, Diagnosis 3: Mortuari* and others. In 2011 and 2021, he was invited as one of the panellists in Singapore's Writers Festival and attended MASTERA literature program at Bogor, Indonesia in 2017. Two of his poems were selected in the literature text-book for *Sijil Pelajaran Malaysia* syllabus. He was the founder of Grup Karyawan Luar Negara which was active in promoting literature and writing among Malaysian overseas students and is currently the owner of Penerbitan Kata-Pilar (Kata-Pilar Books), publishing literature and medical related books. For writings and publications, he has received around fifty awards and literary prizes. This includes four Malaysia Premier Literary Prize (Hadiah Sastera Perdana Malaysia), three National Book Awards (Anugerah Buku Negara), twelve Kumpulan Utusan Literary Prize (Hadiah Sastera Kumpulan Utusan), fourteen Darul Iman Literary Prize (Hadiah Sastera Darul Iman), six E-sastera. com Literary Prize (Hadiah Sastera E-sastera.com), an Islamic Literary Prize (Hadiah Sastera Berunsur Islam) and a Student Literary Prize (Hadiah Sastera Siswa). His book *Menggeledah Nurani* won Best Poetry Book in Hadiah Sastera Darul Iman (2013). His book *Kota Subuh* won ITBM-PENA-BH Writing Competition (2013) and Best Poetry Book in Hadiah Sastera Darul Iman (2015). His short-stories book, *Cinta Menyala di Constantinople* won Best Teen Short-Stories Book in Hadiah Sastera Darul Iman (2017). His novel *Pascasejarah* won the first prize in ITBM-PENA-BH Writing Competition (2015). It also won Best Short-Stories Book in Hadiah Sastera Darul Iman (2017), and was a finalist in Hadiah Sastera Perdana Malaysia (2017).

After Time

Fahd Razy

PENGUIN BOOKS

An imprint of Penguin Random House

PENGUIN BOOKS

USA | Canada | UK | Ireland | Australia
New Zealand | India | South Africa | China | Southeast Asia

Penguin Books is part of the Penguin Random House group of companies
whose addresses can be found at global.penguinrandomhouse.com

Published by Penguin Random House SEA Pte Ltd
9, Changi South Street 3, Level 08-01,
Singapore 486361

Penguin
Random House
SEA

First published in Penguin Books by Penguin Random House SEA 2021
Copyright © Fahd Razy 2022
The author acknowledges the translation of this work
done by Adibah Abdullah

ISBN 9789815017793

Typeset in Garamond by MAP Systems, Bangalore, India

www.penguin.sg

Contents

Foreword

History is said to be the best teacher, but how good were humans at learning their lessons?

On the long road towards culture and sophistication, human beings evolved from tribal barbarians to civilized social creatures From the beginning of time, our history was tainted by lust, envy, and hatred, giving rise to wars and destruction. Civilizations soared and crumbled, only for new nations to emerge from the old ruins. Like a wheel that rotated on the same spot, history never failed to record the same tales. Across time, continents, and oceans. Every nation followed the same narrative, starting from the first murder by the first humans.

What if the continuum is abruptly stopped, a reset button pushed, and the world is given a second chance to restart? With the deeds of the past erased, knowledge became dust, and human beings had to dig their sustenance from the earth—the way our ancestors did when we first began to colonize the land.

Will we, as a species, armed with intelligence and conscience, fare differently then?

After Time speculates on this conjecture—if the *Homo civilis* were forcefully dragged back to point zero, where and how will be their progress henceforth? Will they build and soar to the skies, or will they build and crash again?

The original text, *Pascasejarah,* which literally means 'post-historic', a counter for the phrase 'pre-historic', reflects on how the tales in this book were meant to explore how human beings will continue to persist after the end of history, as we used to know it. Challenging the organic, continuous structure of a novel, *Pascasejarah* was published as a compilation of episodic chapters, each telling an independent story. Every chapter comprised of unique plots and characters, and were linked to each other in a loose chronological fashion. Although this was not made explicit in the narration, clues and traces of links between the chapters were scattered along the way. The reader will be pleased to join the dots and witness how these inter-dependent events culminate in the final event, answering the question posed earlier.

History was said to be the best teacher, but how good were humans at learning their lessons? Can a reset button change anything, or is history not a mere record, but actually a set formula, presented in all the possible variants only to reach the same predictable conclusion?

Pascasejarah, published in Malaysia by ITBM in 2015, has won the first prize for ITBM-PENA-BH Writing Competition (2015). It has also won Darul Iman Literary Prize III as the Best Compilation of Short-Stories.

After Time 1: Apocalypse

'ASK not for what reason I came to exist. Ask instead how they cease to be.'

Birth of civilizations follow the same natural order that, say, a child affirms when she slid out of the womb and began to wail. The wailing cry marked the moment her existence begun. Like a whistle blown to start a race. God has ordained the commandments, the laws of nature. Fire burns. Ice cools. River flows. Apples fall—some of them landed on genius young Newton's nose. Those laws of nature, thus observed, seem so benign, with neither drama nor climax.

'Surely the grasp of gravity didn't bring down a civilization, no?'

It made no sense. Their civilization was beyond powerful. Antibiotics. Vaccines. Nuclear power. Robotics. Nanotics. Supersonics. Digital marks. Satellites. Polymers. Internet. Computer. Electrons. Protons. Facebook. Nay, the jargons of progress crackled like popcorn in a pan: Pop-Pop-Pop! They even capered on the moon's face. Can you believe it?

'Enough. It matters not who am I.'

I was just an effect. The bottom link in the chain of causality. While they, they were the cause, motive, source. And even climax. They were the lessons. While I was the penalty. Yes, I am a tiny dot at the far end of the historic timeline.

(This is beginning to sound drearily academic. Is it?)

Let me tell a story about them. Three G's—Gold, Gospel, Glory. Open the history books and find this imperialist mantra. Together, the three G's brought forth the gravity that pulled civilization down.

The whole of history is not dissimilar to a textbook. Or a guide for idiots. God wrote it all in laughably simple terms, but they never learn. *Homo arrogans*. They never remember their past. Arrogance froze their reasoning in moribund ignorance. Pavlov's dogs or Skinner's mice were smarter. They may not have the capacity for jargon such as 'cause' and 'effect', but they remembered. And they learnt.

Imagine history as carriages of a train. The first class was resplendent with luxury and privacy. The second class consisted of soiled bunk beds. The third class was crowded, dense, and stank with stale perspiration. The cargo car area was loaded with goods. Appetizing aromas wafted from the cafeteria. And forget not the toilets that haven't seen maintenance since the first dump was taken there. Each of the carriages bore their own caste, moved as a separate sect.

(Let's be bombastic and name this train 'hierarchy'.)

Nevertheless, this represents history. The wheels of the different carriages turned on the same rail tracks. Powered by the same locomotive. Riding through the same sequences of sun-rain-drought-storm-quiet-smoke-burn-war. Finally, preeet! For every carriage, the journey eventually ended at the same one station.

'Pardon me for my redundancy. I got carried away a bit—what were we discussing just now? Ah yes. Did you ask me how a glorious civilization fell into rubbles? You might as well ask me how ripe fruits fall.'

The first G—Gold. They are *Homo economicus*.

Gold is the universal dream. Carcinogenic lumps of matter. They divided themselves, multiplying, multiplying like yeasts. Rearing their mouldy heads. Infesting the body of a civilization like a pandemic.

Alexandre Othello was a German-born mineralogist from Central Europe, who graduated in the Northern America. It started with him. It was him, Alexandre, who first discovered a strange ore in an abandoned Ugandan mine. He christened it 'Black Gold'. The material was inert with a sophisticated sheen not unlike polished onyx. When an aurum-carbon compound with an anomalous allotropic composition underwent fission using a simple chemical formulae, Black Gold produced enough power to keep a small town going for a week. Every energy conundrum answered, Black Gold took the topmost seat as the most valuable, sought-after ore.

The Nobel Prize went to Alexandre. So did a professorial chair in an American Ivy League university. As well as research grants worth millions of dollars. And magazine cover photos (plus behind-the-screen, after-the-shoots benefits) with supermodels. Black Gold is the philosopher's stone of the modern world. It gave life, and bred greed. When placed against each other, life of the unwashed masses was no match against the greed of the capitalist giants.

Possessing Black Gold means domination of the world's economic trident. Imagine, Poseidon wearing a capitalist's suit, roaring around the world in a Mercedes. Africa was an almost untapped gold mine, where all the Black Gold lay dormant. Like a virgin waiting to be defiled. Fortunately, its guardians were ignorant people who were far behind in the race towards power, tribes of poor black nomads who punctuated their daily lives with wars and petty fights. The capitalists engineered ways to gain power over the people, with the sole aim of gaining control over the Black Gold.

First, trained spies from secret units were sent on infiltration missions to spark further unrest. Diplomats parroted the slogan, 'Your problem, our problem.' Weapons were sold or given for free. Seeds for civil wars were planted and soon grew with entwining shoots. The hands of the victims completed the dirty work against themselves. Old dictators tumbled down, new dictators took office. The survivors ate scorched sands and drank liquid smoke in refugee camps while staring at circling vultures.

Second, scientists and biotechnologists cooked up fatal virus strains with hidden vaccines and cures. From biohazard labs 100 feet under the ground, the microbes were delivered to Black Gold-laden African countries through contaminated water supplies. Bubonic, haemorrhagic, gangrenous plagues rapidly ravaged the country, eating through the villages and towns, and the handful of cities like uncontrolled forest fire. The initial aim was to merely cull the population to half, but the bug outsmarted its creators. Like every living thing, they wanted to propagate. So they propagated. They crossed continents and cast a darkness known as the 'Black Plague'.

They rode on migrants and refugees escaping across borders. They hitched lifts on rodents and carrion beasts, thus transforming them into pathogen-carrying vectors. Terrified European countries sealed off their sea and air ports. Middle East border posts were equipped with sharpshooters—with orders to eliminate any stragglers upon sight.

Nobody has found a cure. All the vaccines and cures supposedly available during the initial release of the bioweapon were laughed at by the free-running microbes. They have evolved faster than any scientist could predict. Their complexity more staggering than any microbiologist can explain. And they definitely are bigger than any jar can contain.

Africa was quarantined like a huge prison, populated by wandering zombies. 1.1 billion of people, and the mouth-watering reserve of Black Gold lay forgotten. The story of Black Gold, instead of a fairy tale of success, turned into a cautionary tale of greed. First there was Black Gold. Then came the Black Plague. And finally there was an unnamed Black Continent in the latest atlas (if they managed to produce a new one before their civilization spluttered its dying breaths).

'Do not query how I came to know these scraps from the past. My identity is not of importance here.'

The second G—Gospel. They were *Homo religius*. Oh yes they were. Religion was an important part of their lives, until it wasn't.

Every rain drop, stone crack, lightning flash, wave splash, bird twitter, thunder growl—all that moves and grows below the sky was dictated by heavenly decrees. They believed in God. They laid the foundational bricks of their civilization while whispering God's Names. Their nations developed and expanded under the glory of God. They transformed their deserts, steppes, *burrens*, and snowy mountains into robust cities, while remembering to keep God in their hearts, and aspiring to build His paradise on earth.

Soon, religiosity began to feel like a hindrance. Religion was holding them back, so they started to believe. And when the Industrial Revolution boomed—they began worshipping at a new altar, serving tributes to the engines and motors, and sciences. God's new role was a metaphysical product to be priced and sold appropriately.

Faith became disposable cloaks. Mass-produced in factories. Packaged and sold in one-size-fits-all measurements. To be purchased and worn by anyone who wished so. And wore it they did. Politicians and celebrities always made sure that their cloaks of faith look immaculate when making public appearances. Philosophers, authors, and academicians wore their cloaks to increase book sales and talk shows. Military junta remembered to slung the cloaks across their shoulders while slaughtering dissidents. Kept the blood from splattering on their own shirts too.

Dictators and oligarchs led the way towards innovativeness. They reconstructed the cloaks of faith into banners and posters, upon which were written the constitutions of a broken nation, thus convincing the faithful mass to keep them in power.

The bricks fell almost all at once. In the overpopulated South Asia, one tiny dispute over farmland magnified into a feud between families. Then escalated to a conflict between villages. Words and shouts became slashes of knives and swords. And religion became a handy weapon to wield. A bloody interfaith confrontation was the result. Buddhists, Muslims, and Hindus broke each other's necks in front of their prayer houses. In front of their Gods and Lords. The land split into territories of warring religious factions.

The people of West Asia wore uniforms of faith. Flew flags of faith. Flaunted emblems of faith. Rode in vehicles of faith. They put God at the tips of their rifles like a bayonet. While proclaiming that it was God who wanted all the disbelievers and dissenters dead, that it was God who inspired this carnage beneath their feet.

The guns and the bombs were hymns to His glory.

In Tel Aviv, Zionist and Ashkenazis doggedly held onto their determination to destroy the goyims, build their holy temple and establish Eretz Yizrael. Oil tycoons from the Gulf shook each other's hands and kissed each other's cheeks while hiding daggers inside their robes. Power-hungry militants and freedom fighters spoke in the same language, fished for words from the same lexicon. American and European investors, supposedly Christians who declared 'In God We Trust' but had all but forgotten the deeds of Christ, were busy giving dinner parties and toasting warlords while letting offers slip—'. . . by the way, we have a new chemical weapon, we're sure you'd love to give them a try . . . have another champagne?'

Neurotoxin fumes were released in to the atmosphere. The first load of chemical warfare was unleashed from a bomber plane in Tehran. Nature gleefully interfered and sent an unexpected storm, which spread the fumes far till the borders of Lebanon. Casualties piled on top of each other, their sides in the war blurred in the mess of convulsing and rotting bodies. Middle East turned into a fume cupboard saturated with poisonous gases. The rest of the story was too horrendous to narrate.

East Asia and Southeast Asia were men drunken with lust. Religion was their bride adorned with jewellery, lips red, and lashes curled. Shyly beckoning from the marital bed. Their steamy night of passion lasted until daybreak, and calls for the dawn prayer floated ignored in the air as the lovers succumbed to deep-sated sleep. Then for breakfast they were served with stories of religious conspiracies, or religious celebrities. Religious labels were stamped on every secular product. Everyone spoke religion, gave commentaries on it, and dissected the principles, from preschool kids to toothless grandpas.

'Faith is personal. Faith belongs to individuals. The rights to wear, buy, and sell faith is also personal.' So a young uprising politician commented. He was purportedly very keen to show his interfaith goodwill by encouraging believers of all other faiths and none to pray with the Name of his God in their various religious ceremonies.

People had open and covert affairs with religion, they claimed to have so much love and passion for the faith, yet their claims were all but lip service. They were lovers who came during the night full of lust and left in the morning. Without even a farewell.

'Hold on. I haven't finished. These pieces of the time before have always been missing from the records.'

The third G was *glory*. Wait, let me add another G—*girl*.

(Suppress your laughter. This is no jest. Woman is the little David who defeated Goliaths of men. Woman is a bent rib that stabs the heart.)

She was born in Huayin, Shanxi, a rural area deep in the China mainland, not far from the Mongolian border. Her name was Mei, which meant beauty. Her Mongol and Manchu ancestry manifested in her exquisite classic looks. She was born a pauper—her parents were poor farmers with a small plot of land and some livestock. After a fight with several thugs, her parents went missing and Mei was left alone. With no one to work the farm and tend to the animals, and a developer planning to demolish their hut to build railway tracks across the village, Mei decided to seek a better life in the city.

Mei was born to pose and preen, not to break her dainty back or thrash her soft little hands with farm jobs. At the tender age of seventeen, she was one of the most in-demand models in the city. Politicians and businessmen from Hong Kong and Mainland salivated at the sight of her curvy hips and half-open lips. Her provocative poses could bring even a grandpa's flaccid member to life. By the age of twenty-one, she was gracing the side of China's Number Two man. A trophy for a man in the end of his fifties, in whose fingertip hung the fate of 1.4 billion people.

At that tender age Mei became a Republic icon, as the world gazed in admiration. 'Blooming flowers pale in comparison, the full moon dims before her smile,' a Mainland poet gushed. Her elegance enchanted the millions of people, so much that they forgot their hunger and poverty. In reverence they called her Yang Guifei, an 8th century royal beauty.

A larger-than-life statue made of bronze and copper was built. The statue stood gracefully in an honoured spot in the Capital, inscribed on it—Mei 'Yang Guifei', Queen of Modern China. She was the nation's sweetheart, reminding them that in the harsh world beauty and purity still exists. For a while.

Not long after, the angel, the Queen, broke the Republic's heart. She was seen hand-in-hand with an American leader—the people of the devil, enemy of the Republic! The official story was that Mei was kidnapped, but truth was—Mei willingly followed the white General after a successful courtship during a dance. The Republic adoration was stifling, Mei chose to cross the oceans for freedom.

This is a disgrace. An insult. A debasement of our manhood—the Number Two man made his speeches. They challenged us, and we will not cower in fear. What they took wasn't just a woman, but they took the life of the Republic! A new ordinance was passed—any picture, video, any bits of information about Mei on the internet or printed media was forbidden. She was both a victim and an aggressor. The murdered and the murderer. An honour and a dishonour. A name that must remain unspoken.

Seeing two giants at odds with each other, Russia quickly chose to take a side. They never really trusted America since the Cold War, so the lesser of two evils is China. Conflict escalated further when diplomatic bonds were severed. Embassies were closed. The military took up arms. Satellites were poking and peering behind every cloud and wave transmissions.

(Amidst the chaos, nobody really remembered the exact time Mei's bronze-copper statue lost its head).

One fateful night, the American president made a phone call to the Russian president. No one knew the details of the secret conversation, but soon after that, Mei went missing. Five days passed, and her corpse was found frozen in the snow-covered suburbs of Russia. Dress stained black with dried blood from the deep slashes on her neck.

History consisted of repetitive clichés, following simple formulas. Similar to a textbook. Or carriages in a train. After some years passed, China–Russia–America pointed nuclear heads towards each other to avenge the death of a woman—Mei. *Homo sexus. Homo arrogans.* Nay, human beings are the most foolish students of history.

The world turned into an oven, baked crisp with radiation. Holes were punched and torn in the atmosphere. Extreme climate changes shook the globe crazy. Those who did not die in the wars ended as human roasts. Yes, the angry earth roasted them to death.

Their civilization turned into rubble. Dragged down by the gravity that they created. An apple falling from its tree. 3Gs? No, 4Gs.

'After listening to what I have said, you still insist to know why I came to exist?'

Gold, Gospel, Glory, and Girl.

I have told you once, and I will say it again. History was spontaneous, following natural laws. The reset button has been pressed. A new people shall rise from the ruins of those who came before. Crawling out from the depths and becoming the new *Homo civilis*. The wailing cry at the moment of their births was a mark of existence, a whistle blown to start a race.

I am the starting line of a new race.

I am the page in a history book. An empty page to be filled with what humans love to call 'the future'. Call me the post-apocalypse. I like how the phrase rings. Elegant, noir, and a little bit gothic.

You could be more straightforward and call me the time after. I come after history ceased to be, after humanity lost its memory. I am the empty space where the remnants of human beings rose again to build something new from ashes of the past.

I am the era that took place after time as measured by the rise and fall of civilizations cease to be recorded. I am the time after time. Time after time.

The after time.

After Time 2: Chimera

YOU perched on the top of the giant structure, like a gargoyle.

You squinted against the sun. Its unfamiliar rays were ants squirming upon your eyelids. You sniffed the sweet-smelling air; expanded your chest to fully inhale the fresh oxygen. How delicious! You could almost taste the sunshine. Healthy green grass. Cotton-white clouds. The chirping birds. The buzzing insects . . . oh! This is a newborn world, a newborn you. This is paradise—you had forgotten the meaning of that particular word, but it sounded appropriately pleasant, good enough to describe the wonderful sights and scents that you were enjoying.

You stretched your body, relishing the pleasure of straightening and flexing your back, arms, and legs. The muscles have been stiff and bent for so long.

But of course. Twenty-five-odd-years ago you fell down the hole on your own, six-times-six-feet, a blind manhole that led to a labyrinth of sewers. It was so dark, swarming with rats. Littered with debris from hell, it could well have been one of its pits.

The last thing you remembered—the world was crawling on its belly, gasping with its dying breaths. Nuclear warheads clashed in the air, vomiting monstrous fire that roasted the earth to ashes. The sky was ripped open and you saw thick black smoke trying to patch the shredded clouds. You never really knew why the superpower nations were flattening the globe with such bloodlust. Once you read from a piece of food wrapper that used to be a tabloid, that they were murdering each other and the rest of the planet over a queen, an angel on earth. You laughed the doomsayers off, remained optimistic, while trying to imagine her curves and her luscious lips, which apparently were worth blasting bombs for. You couldn't believe it. 'Aren't humans still too wise, to kill and to die just for a woman?'

When the poisonous fog came rushing from the north part of the city, the inhabitants scampered like terrified chickens. The sooty smoke was lethal—inhaling one lungful of it rendered all limbs stiff and brought seizures so intense that bones could break. Eyes bulged red, and blood spurted from the ears and nostrils. Such vivid and three-dimensional deaths have haunted your dreams since the past twenty-five-odd years—those were your final clear memories.

Today, you finally saw the earth after its rebirth. You stood alone, on top of a giant structure. Perched like a gargoyle statue. There was no coincidence.

You were convinced of this miracle. God chose you Himself. Selected to continue the survival of humanity. He threw you in the dark hole just to keep you safe. To keep your superior genetics alive, so you could pass it to your descendants. You were going to father a new generation of humans. The *Homo ultimatus*. An invincible species undefeated by wars and disasters. Charles Darwin would have cited this as an evidence of nature making her selection, and you were the chosen patriarch!

You stretched and tried to straighten your back properly—again. You failed—again. You fell on your fours—again. You couldn't stand straight on two legs, not anymore.

The quarter-century spent in the narrow labyrinths have transformed your physique. The back was crushed into a perpetually forward bent, and you weren't walking. You crawled on all fours— like a gibbon, or an orangutan. Darwin would have described this as a post-historic evolution. You knew his theories were mostly bluffs, but you worshipped him anyway. You used to say that only those who successfully adapt were going to proceed in climbing the stepladder of survival. His words now promised a euphoric hope for the dispossessed, dehumanized you. Look, the filthy scruffy hair growing over your whole body after the irradiation of your follicles, dermis and melanin. Your skin took a dirty charred tone. Coarse to touch. While your back and scalp were covered in patches of crusty scabs.

O new world! Here I come to conquer—you were excited, imagining how Caesar approached Zela, proclaiming *veni, vidi, vici.* You rushed down the mounds of broken concrete, sharp at the multiple edges, rough and craggy. Your senses were sharper—that must have been another blessing evolution has granted. With your strong and solid leg muscles, you leapt far across, to the other side of the ruins.

You began to wander around. Exploring the post-historic world after twenty-five-odd cursed years. Was not this place used to be a metropolis, while you were a vermin crawling on its pavements together with the rest of the civilizational trash. This once-city had been a giant coliseum where you had to face barbaric battles with a multi-headed monster called Life. With no shield. No sword. Blindfolded and hands bound. Onlookers laughed as you were pounded, writhing and thrashing. Struggling to get up. That was what you were—a show animal, whose purpose was to entertain the capitalists, economists, and political royalties on the viewers' seats. They could barely control their excitement. They couldn't wait to cheer for the finale when you would finally be wrestled to death.

No. You didn't die. They never watched you fall to your death. Now you were the one laughing. And you were going to forefather a new civilization.

You leapt swiftly from one clearing to another. You climbed and broke through ruins, rubbles, and decapitated pillars, heaps of misshapen concrete chunks that used to be banks and luxury emporiums. You scrounged for something edible. You need to survive. Your belly was growling louder, reminding you that since exiting the ghastly pits, you haven't had any morsel to eat.

You saw something glinting beneath the gravelly sand, and picked it up. A strange metallic object. Silvery grey. Your curious fingers clumsily pressed and rolled the small wheel-shaped part—the only part that you could move on the object. A bit stiff, but it was turning. You pressed and turned it again, faster, faster. And pop! A small reddish warm tongue of flame spluttered out from a tiny hole.

You had forgotten how a lighter looked like and how it worked, but now you remembered. The flame was beautiful, enchanting. You haven't seen fire for so long—and this one danced in front of you so gracefully. You could almost feel a cigarette waiting to be lit. You extinguished the flame (you knew you can bring it back) and kept the lighter in your person, it was going to be useful.

Crawling and leaping. Leaping and crawling and swinging. Until you arrived to a greener valley. A delicious aroma wafted from the area, that smell beckoned you there. A luscious tempting scent. You finally saw where the aroma came from—a wide expanse of banana trees. Banana trees bent with ripe bunches, each fruit twice larger than bananas you remembered from the old days. Salivating, you leapt forward, grabbing a hold on the nearest low bunch, snapped it off the tree.

You ate the manna from heaven. Wasn't the world purged of its past, for you to start a new story? Everything was meant for you now. Goodbye ghettoes of the past, welcome paradise of the future! Nuclear wars scorched the land, turning the earth into a graveyard. From its ashes rose a fertile new world. A new world populated with the most beautiful, the most delicious things. Like the bananas you're gobbling now. The most delightful food you have had. In the dark pits food was anything you could hold, anything you could bite and chew. You didn't know what half of those food were. You never wanted to know. Some squeaked. Some didn't make any sound. Some were slimy and scaly. Hunger didn't allow you the luxury to be picky.

The food kept you engrossed. You never noticed the eyes watching from afar, and you definitely weren't aware of them approaching. There were several of them. Only until their shadows blocked the sun, you noticed that something was amiss—but it was too late. A thump on the back sent you tumbling face first onto the pebbly soil.

'This is my territory! Everything that grows and falls here goes under my say-so!'

You lifted your head to see the originator of the cursed voice, wetly hoarse and stuttering, who was standing before you. Standing on his fours. His body must be like yours—as much as you could discern without a mirror—overgrown with coarse long hair. Only difference was the greyish-white hair on his chest, making him look distinguished and probably charismatic, although this man must be at least half your age.

He was surrounded by similar figures, who looked far sturdier and more masculine. The nearest one, whose head was almost fully covered with red hair, held a gritty stone club. Your head must have been bludgeoned by that.

'How would I know that?' you snapped in reply.

Their response was another hit from the stone club, this time pounding your right shoulder. You were thrown to the left, unable to get up. The red-headed man lifted his club, directly above your head. Did you survive twenty-five years in hell only to get your head bashed to death here?

'Stop,' the white-chested man ordered. He crawled forward, while the rest moved back. He clearly held the most power, despite his smallest size.

'I am the Ruler. This is my territory,' he repeated. 'New guy, I don't want you to die just yet. I hope you're going to be useful to me soon.' His smile was honeyed, and had edges to it. The smile of a man in power—the kind of smile you knew so well. That was the smile you saw carved across the faces of the audience who cheered when you were being murdered in the coliseum—while fighting life. There was no choice. You nodded, swallowing all bitterness. To live was more important.

They lifted you and dragged you. Both of your arms were held by brawny men, while your legs lugged along like dead weights. You closed your eyes in pain and exhaustion, but kept your ears perked. Grass beneath you grew thicker and coarser. While the bird chirps were gradually replaced by loud buzzing of crickets. You were entering the forest. The sun's glare grew weaker, less burning on your back. Afternoon already gave way to evening, while night-time was waiting for its turn nearby. The group was moving faster, while heaving your weak injured body.

'Quick. It's almost night. We must not bump into him.' You heard the Ruler's wetly hoarse voice. He sounded stern and worried. 'Soon it will be his hunting time.'

'Who will be hunting?' You couldn't contain your curiosity. For a moment, your question hung in the air unanswered. The group focused on moving, now even faster.

'Shhh. Don't say his name out loud. Brings bad luck.' The man who was hauling your right arm half-whispered, almost out of breath in their hurry. 'It's a mutated beast. Probably got hit by radiation. Ate flesh, both dead and alive. We called it...shh...*chimera.*'

You remained silent with eyes closed, but kept listening.

'When the sky gets really dark, he will come out to hunt. We must reach the settlements quick, or we are going to be his dinner,' the man on your left added. 'The creature was God's punishment to us. After twenty-five years, we were still too sinful to be forgiven.'

You opened your eyes when the pace became slower. You heard more whispering voices. Before you, laid a settlement of caves, carved into limestone rocks. In the dimming light you counted the people swarming around, about sixty of them. A settlement. A colony. You never thought that there were still humans left over in the world.

'The first human city,' you mumbled, while beginning to plant an ambition.

They left you leaning against a large rock. You watched the people anxiously running here and there, trying to close a cave mouth. Some of them were trying to lift huge stones.

'You're going to be with me,' the White-chested Ruler squatted next to you. 'I have a deep cave with a small entrance. The beast could not come in. All the other caves were too wide, too shallow. Not enough to save them. Not when the dark has fallen.'

'So why were they still hiding there, if those caves couldn't protect them from the beast?'

'I don't know. Perhaps they were entertaining themselves of their own false hopes.'

'Let them all enter the deep cave, where you said the beast could not enter.'

'I'm the Ruler. How could I share the same hole with them? Eventually, someone must be sacrificed to keep the others alive, right? Let nature take its course.' The Ruler snickered. His rasping voice reminded you of a seal yelping. He reminded you so much of the elitists whose snickers and yelps have tortured you before the disaster silenced all of them.

'I shall kill the beast!' you raised your voice, purposefully challenging the man. The white-chested ruler seemed astonished. The other people nearby heard your voice. Heard the impossible suggestion, and turned to watch.

'I know why the *chimera* was a nocturnal beast, why he appeared only at night, and I have a weapon to counter it!'

'How?' a woman eagerly asked.

'No one could kill the monster. Don't you think we have tried multiple times already?' another person, a man, butted in.

The Ruler remained silent, either considering your proposal, or still finding it too shocking. You took out the lighter and stared at him. 'If I were successful, I want half of the banana plantation.'

'If you fail?' the Ruler's eyes widened in response to the blatant challenge.

'I will be dinner for the beast tonight!'

The hillsides buzzed with noise. The sun was sinking. Shadows were getting longer before dissolving altogether into the homogenous dark. The Ruler remained silent, pulled back and slowly crawled into his cave.

'There should be no harm in trying. If you failed, at the very least, we are assured of a sacrifice tonight.'

'How tall is the beast?' you asked the red-headed man holding his trusty club.

'Three times an adult man.'

'How long?'

'Five times.'

'How far does it leap?'

'*Chimera* doesn't leap.'

'So, it crawls? Slithers? Like a snake?'

'No, not a snake. It's more like a big lizard.'

'Can it climb?'

The man shook his head. You sniffed the lighter, arranging your thoughts.

Then you summoned ten of the strongest-looking men and you told them the trick you've concocted. There were many things to get done, before night completely fell. They went their separate ways straightaway and returned almost immediately, their arms laden with dried leaves and sticks. Heaped into piles as you had planned.

The Ruler took multiple glimpses of what was going on, from where he was staying in his cave. He must be worrying about the soon-to-be-lost half of the banana plantation. If you can beat such a ferocious beast, certainly it wouldn't take much for you to defeat him, the white-chested Ruler. You will gather your own followers in no time.

'O Ruler, stay in your cave, don't leave, just observe. You'll get good view from inside the cave. I will be the bait!' you shouted.

Night fell and moon rose. You climbed up the stone hill and crouched on its top. Waiting for the beast. The other humans were hiding, shivering in their caves. Hugging each other for warmth, or perhaps for some courage to cushion their fears.

The swollen moon was leisurely making its way up the sky, and underneath its dim glow, you saw shadows.

You smelled a thick, biting stench. Like that of a carcass. Not much worse though than what you were used to in the labyrinths. It pounded its way towards you in noisy, clumsy steps. Trees shook when its bulk crashed against them. The predator was showing its arrogance—standing at the top of the food pyramid, it does not need to bother hiding its presence. The appearance of the beast itself is the arrival of impending death.

A ferocious face, a pair of fangs, long neck, and branched snake-like tongue. Six legs. A second head on its back, resembled a crocodile, with two horns sticking on top. The legs were covered in shiny scales, while the bulk of the body was obscured by thick gristly fur. Killing intent emanated from its every motion. You trembled without even realising it. Yet your determination and thirst for power overcame all fear.

'Twenty feet from the hill,' you begun yelling and screaming. Trying to attract the beast's attention. It worked. The thing stopped in its tracks. It stared at you on top of the hill, piercing you with its bloodthirsty gaze. After several long moments, it gave a monstrous bellow and raced towards you.

The people watching from their caves held their breaths, including the Ruler. Fear took their voices and almost chased their hearts out of their chests.

The beast grated its claws against the rocks, trying to climb. But the claws were too long and pointed, not suitable for mounting its weight. It wailed and bellowed in desperation. The forest was silent except for the hollering of the beast.

'Now!' you yelled.

Ten men stealthily approached from afar, pressed the lighter you gave, and hey presto! Ten torches flared up. Heaps of dried leaves, piled in multiple directions, quickly caught fire, forming a flaming partial ring against the rocky hills, between which the hungry beast was trapped. The beast went frantic. Its eyes couldn't bear the light. Its hide could stand no heat. The thing bellowed and thrashed desperately, as the burning ring crept closer, and finally grilled it alive.

After what felt like forever, it stopped struggling. And perhaps stopped breathing, too. The final tongues of flames took their time. Slowly licking the carcass with soft crackling sounds.

'Help! I couldn't get out!' said the ugly voice, wet and hoarse. And squeaky like a seal, startled everybody. It was followed by a painful cough. You laughed—a deep, satisfied belly laugh.

'Why did you obey a stupid ruler?' you hollered from the top of the hill, while swinging the stone club. Sparks of fire appeared where it hit the rocks. 'He was too young when the twenty-five-year-ago disaster happened. How old was he then, three, four years old? He didn't even know what is fire or smoke! How could he lead a civilization?'

You gazed upon the sixty-odd people standing below. For the first time since a long while, you felt satisfied, like a Caesar who left his bed in the morning and opened his window, looking over as the territories under his rule woke up under the rising sun. Is this how it feels like to have power?

The Ruler was getting weaker. The entry to his cave was barricaded with fire, while smoke poured into it. Suffocating him. Finally he collapsed and fell silent, granting what felt like the power of God into your hands. You barely had a few seconds to visualise the empire you were going to build when a *chimera* pounced onto your back. Blood gushed and splattered.

You didn't even have the time to scream. At least the rats in the labyrinth managed to squeak as you bit into their necks.

You disappeared into the darkness. The people below the hill were stunned, frightened, unsure what to do. A mumble rose.

The sturdy red-headed man came forward. 'The idiot didn't know that there are two *chimera*s. Don't worry. The beast wouldn't ravage us tonight, not with a full belly. Tomorrow night, we shall kill it.'

'How are we going to kill the thing? We have no fire!'

The man picked up the club that you dropped, and swung it against the rocks until fire sparked. All the others watched in amazement.

'I can bring forth fire from rocks,' he smiled. 'Today onwards, this colony belongs to me. Call me the Red-Headed Ruler,' he roared.

Deep in the forest, your unseeing eyes gazed towards the stars.

Beneath the moonlight. Beneath the sprinkles of stars, your belly was torn open and its contents chomped with wet slopping sounds.

After Time 3: The Dream

IT used to be a massive emporium, the only remnant of the past civilization that still remained intact. The walls were polished, looking luxurious with decorations from skin, teeth, bones, and horns from successful hunts. The milk-white marble floor, lined with carpets weaved from animal fur. Green and yellow herbs arranged to surround the hall—symbol of prosperity and wealth. What a ceremonial hall! Fit for a Sovereign Ruler.

You froze after the third step. No. This was not your first time entering the hall. But you never looked at it with your physical sight. Now you actually were looking at it, you could see how the display was a blatant material-arrogance. The conceit glared at you, piercing your eyes.

This palace has been so familiar to your senses since you were proclaimed the Great Laureate, a status at par with an Empire advisor. You knew the location of the door and throne. The number of steps on the stairway. Where the pillars were. Where the guards and governors and advisors were positioned. The windows from which the sounds of birds and smells of shrubs floated into the hall. And the torches which lent their heat (and light, which you couldn't appreciate yet at that time). Almost like an architect, every inch and specification of the space was part of the schematic embedded in your head.

The only thing you haven't seen with your eyes was the truth. Truth for you were blanketed in dreams and darkness.

Every two to three weeks you would pay your visit, entertaining the Ruler with your dreams and prophecies. Occasionally you would wax lyrics with philosophies and predictions for the future. You were an eccentric blind man, blessed (or cursed?) with a miraculous gift. Your blindness (normally would led you to be cast out of society)– ironically became a source of wealth and power, bequeathed to you from the hands of the Ruler.

When you were small, you remember lying on your mother's chest, which was quaking with her sobs. Perhaps you were nine–ten years old then. Mother wept so hard, blaming herself. Her lack of insight led to your lack of sight. When she was carrying you in her womb, she chain-smoked. She took pills to make her happy. Pills to ease her pain. Pills to ease her giddiness and nausea. Pills, herbs, fumes became poisons that rendered her blood toxic, the blood which then went to nourish you inside her. You were born blind. Probably caused by the drugs. Probably by nine months stewing in your mother's messed-up inner chambers.

The twenty-five-years-old apocalypse separated you from her. You never knew for sure how she died. She must've gone the way so many others went—eaten alive by disease and malnutrition. Or her brains ravaged by psychosis and starvation. Somehow you were saved, trapped in a bunker 30 feet underground, with hundreds of other people.

There was no light in the bunker, and having a pair of eyes never helped. Your blindness became an advantage, for the reason that it gave you the most experience with darkness, compared with the others. You navigated your world by touch and hearing. And pure instincts. The makeshift social system in the dark bunker placed you at the top of the pyramid. You had the quickest movements. You were the fastest to catch food. The other humans hung their hopes on you. You explored the ventilation shafts and plumbing ways down there, revelling in the realization that curses could turn into blessings in the blink of an eye. You reached adulthood in the dark bunker, secure and independent in a lightless world.

Your evolution begun in the bunker, and when it happened, it was magical. Slowly your spiritual eyes opened, and you began getting visions of the outside world. You saw images, projections, which you initially thought were hallucinations. You thought you were finally losing your mind. It must be the prolonged entrapment chipping away at your sanity, or pieces of your mother's unfortunate genetics—but you were wrong.

The first vision you saw was that of a woman. A beautiful woman with petite figure and fragile limbs. Her skin was sallow, missing the rosy glow of health. Wrinkles of her life manifested on her forehead and the corners of her sunken eyes. You knew it was your mother. You knew her smile, you could taste its honey. You felt such overwhelming love, you wept uncontrollably. Your second vision was your own self as a child, together with your mother, and two or three friends—all of whom were swallowed by the apocalypse. The nostalgia poured like rain in your mind. Soothing your worries and filling you with feelings of longing. The visions appeared to you like dreams—or were they hallucinations of a madman?

The next visions were more random, more obvious in their mystic. You were blind, but you could see the physical world. Trees, green. Mountains, blue. The ocean, stretching wide to the horizon. Birds. Stars. The moon, swollen and glowing. Sharp gritty rocks. And post-historic humans, crawling and evolving. You saw the film roll unwinding, projecting image upon image onto your dreams—which came when you were asleep or awake (not that there were much difference either way).

The door shut with a startling bang.

You walked to the centre of the great hall. Slowly, fumbling, like you always do, like a blind Great Laureate was supposed to move. No one must know about this new change. No, it must remain a secret, especially since the strange dreams begun haunting you. Since the past six months, since you gained the love and trust of the Ruler. And since your unseeing eyes started to see more, the strange dream recurred like an unsettling ritual. You knew the dream was a skeleton unearthed, a secret exposed, a disaster predicted. You knew your visions never lie. You fear its truth.

'Welcome, o blind poet with miraculous visions,' the Sovereign Ruler's voice roared from his throne. 'I missed your prophecies, it has been three long weeks,' his laughter boomed across the hall, echoed by the walls. You smiled, and stared at the Ruler, relishing your sight of him. This is the first time you saw his features clearly. He was sturdy and muscular. His body was covered with well-groomed hair, clothed with regal attire and adorned with golden ornaments. A silver goblet, shone by his right hand, no doubt filled with a lush royal beverage. His face was young, angular and wide-jawed, befitting his power and leadership. When he smiled, you could see his left canine tooth protruding. A predator's smile.

The Sovereign Ruler was the second-generation ruler of this new empire after his father, Red-Headed Ruler died in a mountain accident. His father was famous as the founder of this nation, after killing a carnivorous monster called a *chimera*. That was what the legends say. He was also the first to discover how to make fire which lit the way for the post-historic society to prosper. The Ruler's eldest brother was also known as a smart administrator, credited for the construction and management of the capital city. Unfortunately he did not live long either—he died in his sleep, apparently consumed by grief after the accident that befell his father, the Red-Headed Ruler.

After taking over the throne, the Sovereign Ruler was often angry and ill-tempered. His way towards supremacy as a ruler was not smooth. The throne was challenged by a series of rebellions, some appearing from the most unexpected places. The Ruler was confused and offended. He felt trapped. The throne was not something a person can simply let go and hand over to someone else without suffering dire consequences. Once he held it, he must continue holding on to it.

One morning, six months ago, the Ruler approached you with an astonishing request.

Normally, you would sit on a mossy tree stump, your humble seat as the Blind Seer. That was the name they called you—once your visions became phenomenal, and the people sought your counsel, the blind man who could see. Every day you would climb up the tree stump, decked with giant orange fungus, growing in a stair-like arrangement. Crowds of post-evolution humans would have been gathering since sunrise. Their eyes shone with expectation, waiting for miracles to be displayed. You would start by scratching your back, where dark long hair grew in frizzles. Then you took your seat and spoke about the visions that arrived behind your eyes.

You spoke about history. The past, the time before. How parasitic oligarchs and rulers with iron fists fought each other over Black Gold, over women, and finally fell to their doom. You also spoke about the future. You could see both ways. A dam would be built, and an amphitheatre would soon stand. You saw a three-headed monster. A one-eyed warmonger. A war that would soon take place against the western kingdom. A strange tale of an advisor who was pushed by hunger to slice off his body parts for dinner. The people gaped in amazement, perhaps more in confusion.

Speculative and provocative whispers spread among your audience. They couldn't believe how a man born blind could know those stories and preach those morals. They couldn't believe your eloquence. They found themselves sceptical, but they were captivated against their own reasoning. You weave such amazing tales, with the most beautiful descriptions. You spoke of the waves that crashed against the shore; of the sun, whose rays warm the blood and stung the skin; of the moon hanging askew under the roof of the world; of white mornings laced with mist. Your way with words embellished what was already beautiful, enhanced the dramatics and kept your audience enthralled. The pictures you showed them were more glorious than what their own eyes could see; they closed their eyes and let themselves sink in your intoxicating yarns.

But some still question aloud.

'Is he truly blind?'

Their scepticism took two of your fingers.

A cynic placed a sharpened piece of coral rock, right in the midst of your path up the tree-stump. According to his logic, this pretentious blind man will be forced to break his cover when he avoided the rock. Your fingers were sliced to the bone, festered for three weeks and finally had to come off. You lost your fingers, but gained more followers with unwavering faith. The cynic lost. Your reputation as *Homo magicus* spread across the lands, eventually arriving in the halls of the Ruler, and brought the man himself before your tree-stump.

'Were you born blind?' The Sovereign Ruler asked.

'I can see without light. My physical eyes were prison bars. My true sight lies in my dreams and visions.'

'How true are your visions?'

'My Lord, help me prove they are not true.'

'How? Have you seen me in your visions?'

'No, but I saw that by midnight a clandestine meeting will take place between five of your trusted governors, in a chamber near the palace kitchens. They will be planning to stab your back.'

The Sovereign Ruler was shocked, and his initial response was disbelief. But such a massive threat, even coming from a blind man (who could be a madman, for all he knew), could not be left unattended. He rushed home to his palace, summoned his best spies to investigate and apprehend.

Before the crowds arrived to surround the mossy tree-stump the next morning, the Ruler came and offered something that you had not foreseen. Yes, you saw the future regularly, but this part never appeared in your visions.

'You will be one of my right-hand men, and I shall proclaim you the Great Laureate. You have no need of this rotten podium. I have prepared a stage for you, special for you, in the city centre, where your revellers can come from all over the Empire. I have arranged everything for you—food, property, residence, maids and servants—all that you could possibly need.'

'What is this for, o Ruler?' Your alarm bells were ringing so loud, this was too sudden for your comfort.

'You must say good things about me. Keep the people loyal, make them worship me as they do you.'

'You never appeared in my visions, o Lord.'

'You have a glib tongue and a bright mind. If I never appeared in your visions, then create a picture of me for the people to see. Make me a hero in your tales. Like the gods in the legends, living in mythical palaces on high mountains where no humans ever set their eyes. I am their king. Their ruler. Their warrior. Brave, clever, wise, and strong. For the sake of the city, the Empire. For the sake of harmony. Everyone will benefit.'

The Sovereign Ruler was persuading you, with urgency that bordered on coercion.

You were in a dilemma. You were being asked to lie, your conscience said that this is not right. Nevertheless, the Ruler was right about the need for harmony. You have seen it—so much bloodbaths in the time that has passed, and in the time yet to come.

'Every two or three weeks, pay your visit to the palace. Tell me about your latest visions. Of the beautiful moon and the gentle sun, or of threatening enemies. Anything you would like to tell me, I would listen. Tell me anything,' the Ruler's voice regained its warmth.

You did not take long to agree. His offers were too good, efforts demanded of you too little. Since then, you learnt to be a propagandist. You spoke for the Ruler. You began spinning grandiose tales about the Ruler, tales that you know were composed of untruths. The Ruler gained more respect and fear from the people, and your social stature raised higher.

As the made-up tales spread further, your physical sight gradually brightened. Initially it was blurry, only bursts of light that sometimes were painful. But the more you spoke of the Ruler, the clearer your sight became. Perhaps there were truths in your yarns—the Ruler indeed descended from noble blood, glorifying him brought blessings upon you, curing your sight. Real, tangible images formed before your eyes. Blurry-blurry-bright. Blurry-bright-bright. And finally, two weeks ago, your vision was truly bright—you were seeing with your pair of eyes like they had never been blind before.

'Why are you silent? Tell me what you have seen.' The Ruler was losing his patience. For a split second, you lost your composure. You averted your gaze, making sure your stare is blank and glazed, preventing the Ruler's suspicion. This man was meticulous and wary, you must not miss your steps.

'What have you dreamt about lately?' The Ruler pushed further, while munching on a large berry.

'I see the Empire expanding, increasing in its prosperity. From the west to the east.'

That caught the Ruler's fancy. He laughed. 'Come on, tell me something I did not already know.'

'The Empire will fall, too. Every civilization in history has followed the same pattern. Once it reached the top, it will stay there for a while, then slid downwards. This will happen—not in your time, not in your son's or your grandson's time. But this will still happen.' You stuttered and stumbled, your usual eloquence had deserted you. 'The Empire will drown in a massive flood, caused by an act of treachery. All of her people and her treasures will sink to the bottom.'

'Write this down, and save it in the national archives. I hope the future successors to the throne would pay attention to it.' The Ruler ordered. 'Now tell me about the past, o wise Blind Seer. Tell me what historic truths were unravelled by your mystical vision.'

'There is this dream—I kept seeing it. It kept coming, and I kept thinking of it. But I couldn't interpret its meaning.' You stopped, and stared at your trembling thumb. You didn't feel that telling this to the Ruler would lead to good endings, but you didn't think keeping it a secret was going to be any better.

'I saw it since the past six months; it recurred again and again. Since I started to enter the palace and served you, Sovereign Ruler.'

'That makes it even more interesting. It must be an important vision. Tell me all of it,' the Ruler was obviously excited.

'I saw a king, going with his youngest son in a hunt. He told his son about his ambitions to build an empire. He confided about his worries— he knew the noblemen in his court and his apparent followers were going to double-cross him sooner or later. I remembered his words: 'This power has given me no joy, it gave me nothing but fear and worry. The palace is a prison filled with gold and riches beyond imagination. The prison door is wide open—but I couldn't walk out. I chose to stay behind bars with the treasures I love too much.'

The Sovereign Ruler was silent, his expression changing. You quickly averted your gaze—yours must not meet his eyes.

'As they walked on a mountain pass, the son asked. 'O father, what would free you from this prison?' The father was quiet for a while before answering. 'Death.' Suddenly the son pushed his father into the gorge. Huge sharp rocks jutted at the bottom. The young prince watched from the top, looked at the now-dead King lying motionless among the rocks, his head smashed and his limbs broken. 'I freed you, father.'

You controlled your agitation, took a deep breath, and continued the story. You could feel the Ruler's eyes drilling a hole into your very being.

'Upon their return to the palace, the youngest prince told his brother that their father unfortunately lost his footing and died. The entire palace was shaken with grief. The King's body was retrieved and buried on top of a hill. On the third night of mourning after the funeral, the youngest prince poisoned his brother's drink with *Zakum* herb. He went to bed and never woke up.'

'When did this happen?' If looks could kill, the Ruler's glare would have strangled you lifeless.

'I do not know,' you shifted in your seat.

'What was the name of the king, and who was the son?' The Ruler pressured further.

'I do not know that either,' your words were almost inaudible in your nervousness. Your heart was leaping out of your chest. You knew it was a mistake. You shouldn't have told the dream to anyone, least of all the Ruler.

The Sovereign Ruler let out a long breath and leaned back against his throne, but his unease was clear. Usually he would conclude the meetings with feasts of meat and juicy fruits, and bade you goodbye with gifts of gold and expensive attire. Now, you were dismissed without ceremony. Not wishing to overstay your welcome either, you crawled out the door. That might be one of your many wrongdoings— you forgot that the Ruler was still watching you for any suspicious signs—and your hurry to leave the hall was obvious.

Once out of the palace, you heaved sighs of relief. You barely escaped with your life, and now your next step—easier with your newfound sight—was to leave the city. To wait even a second longer was to court certain death. Indeed, barely a second later, your head was bundled into a rough black cloth from behind, and multiple beatings subdued you into a helpless crouch. They tied you up and dragged you to your feet. You could hear soldiers bickering and shouting, then sounds of clanging irons. You were dragged across gritty roads, then muddy paths into the jungle.

You didn't recall when did you fall unconscious, but when you opened your eyes, they had removed the black cloth and bound you to a tree trunk. Night was thick and dark, but your eyes still allowed you to see shrubs and bushes around, aided by the slivers of moonlight that broke between cracks in the canopy overhead. There was no other source of light or fire. No sign of civilization. No other human beings other than several soldiers surrounding you. A nearby stream gurgled softly.

'Pardon me, Blind Seer. Pardon us all. The Ruler ordered us to do this.' The nearest soldier spoke. They still had some respect and awe towards you.

'What order? What did he tell you to do?'

'To make sure you were truly blind, and to keep you that way.'

The soldier revealed a piece of wood, two thumbs wide, branch taken off a tree, with one end sharpened to a sharp point. Any words you could have said were lost in your shock and fear. The visions that haunted you for the past six months replayed themselves—the images, the conversations, unfolded in eerie clarity. The visage of the King, his head covered in red hair, and his young son, with angular, wide jaw, so finely chiselled, thrusted themselves upon your eyes.

You were blind, even after you regained your sight.

'Thank you, truth!' the bitter words cursed the miracle that you used to be so grateful for—eyes that could see.

All your dreams and visions dissipated into nothingness once the sharp stick touched your eyes.

After Time 4: The Scholar

IT was a time of despair. You were mad to accept the ruling mandate while the Empire was in chaos.

The previous ruler was a softy. He had always been too weak for his own good. He died by the poison of his own mixing, how pathetic was that? You stopped calling him father out of embarrassment. He chose a humiliating way to die, thus cursing his son with the legacy of a failed man. His mistakes were tattooed on your face for all to jeer at. His failures stained your blood black. Inferior hands raised you to adulthood. Those hands gave you nothing but stunted growth, incompetence, and depression. You cursed. You cursed the previous ruler, and all the wreckage that he left for you.

The wrecks include these three advisors. Three stupid sycophants, kneeling in what they might think as dutiful reverence, but to your eyes they were more like rotten stumps. Of course they were afraid of your rage, waiting for it to subside.

'Say it again, young man!' You swung your sword of gold, symbol of the Empire, slashing the air. The sword was not a ceremonial weapon, it had savoured the blood of enemies. You could aim the edge a certain way, and the young man would be headless. The guard dogs can take their pick of the remains. Those beasts tend to prefer the torso. Arms and legs tend to be rather meatless.

'I would like to offer my help to solve the problems of your Empire, Sovereign Ruler,' the young man spoke in a steady tone. He didn't quiver at the sight of the bloodthirsty sword. You reluctantly gave him credit for courage. He definitely had more guts than the advisors and the governor, those rotten stumps in the Great Hall. You sheathed the sword, and sat on the throne.

'Farmers in the North were starving. The past seven months were hell-sent. No rain, not a drop. We might as well live in the desert and squeeze the rocks for water. Crops withered and died. Livestock became carcasses.' You knew you were merely reiterating facts, miserable facts, that everyone in the Great Hall and beyond knew. The Empire was dying of thirst. Driven by your own eloquence, encouraged by a new audience in the brazen young man, you continued your speech.

'In the South, survival was equally difficult. The people had to take shelter in ruins from the time before, and in dark musty caves. And, and, and . . . the ungrateful things, they dared to blame the Empire for their bad luck. I received news that they were concocting an uprising against me. With what little resources they still had, they dared to make plans to overthrow me!'

'I am aware of that, Sovereign Ruler, and I will help you deal with them. You will win over them, overpower them, and win their loyalties.' The young man was so self-assured you couldn't help but feel amazed. He might not end up as the dogs' lunch after all.

His physique told all about his humble origins. The young man must have been born a peasant. Definitely no wealth where he came from, let alone nobility. The bones jutted from his cheeks and elbows. Where the rags he wore as a shirt was torn, you could clearly see his protruding ribs. Heavy dark circles hung around his eyes. His right forearm was missing, and the scrawny fingers of his one good hand looked like bony claws. Maybe this was just a crazy street kid, hunger snapping his reason, leading him to desperately make an absurd offer in a bid to get food.

You might be just as mad as he was. You let this beggar-kid into the palace, and admit it, you did hope that he really had the answer to the economic-social-political-internal issues of the Empire. If he were mad, you weren't too sane either.

You knew you had good excuse to lose your sanity. The Empire has been in this disarray for decades, since the time of the previous ruler (you would not, would never, call him 'father'). The three advisors were there from the beginning. And they did a fat lot of good. Greed and avarice, and extravagance, as well as perpetual conflicts, have drained the palatial treasury to the last coin. The repositories of the Empire were scraped to the last grain. You, on whose shoulders these ruins were dumped, deserved the right to be insane. Perhaps in the dark recesses of the mind, you could finally lose yourself and take a good, long rest.

From those recesses of your mind, one particular memory came forth, one that you cringed to remember. There was a time when you felt desperate enough, that you asked the three advisors for their wisdom. How, o Advisors, how do we heal this dying Empire?

'Let us increase the tax rate. A portion from every ripe stalk of rice, every cob of corn, every bunch of berries, and not forgetting the juicy bananas, must be given to the palace,' the Development Advisor said. 'We shall keep the collections in the palace treasury, they can feed us for seven generations or more. The people of this country have been too lazy, mollycoddled for so long, that's why we're in such a rut . . . they must work, once they reach twelve years old, they should go out in the fields, no reason why they should pretend to be children . . . '

He couldn't finish his words because of the kick you aimed at his left ribs. The useless lump of meat rolled breathless on the floor, cradling his side, trembling.

'The people will just as soon kick me off the throne, and I will be on the floor like you are now! By then your bones would be dog-munching toys, and your tongue would be used to hang your head by the palace door!'

The second advisor, the Trades Advisor glanced at his fallen comrade. Gulped and mumbled an answer.

'Sovereign Ruler, why don't we build a massive vessel, a merchant's vessel. Make it luxurious, such that those who see it wonder at our wealth. We should carry all our Empire produce and trade with the other Empires. I heard of a new prosperous kingdom in the West. We can build a good business relationship with them.' He actually dared to look smug, thinking that he has finally hit the jackpot.

'We have nothing left to trade, idiot! Going to the West with an empty vessel is only going to expose our poverty, how frail we have become. The Western kingdom will immediately see this as an opportunity to invade us!'

The Trades Advisor curled into the foetal position on the floor, gasping, after your well-placed kick.

The Defence Advisor knew that another kick is going to land on his belly. His face flushed with desperation, eyes closed and with shuddering voice, he suggested, ' . . . why not, why not we attack and conquer the Western kingdom instead?'

You were stunned with the total, unspeakable, indescribable idiocy of the comment. No energy left to kick or hit anyone, you slumped on your throne. Rotten stumps, the three of them. Since that day, they have never shown any joy when attending your royal assemblies. They dared not to, and you know they don't deserve to feel any joy. They were failures. You told the young man exactly that.

'We were all at a dead end. Voice it out, young man. If this is all a waste of time, you are going to be fed to my hungry pets.'

'Sovereign Ruler, in the history of civilization, a lot of empires borne out of successful agricultural and animal husbandry, not unlike this Empire of ours. These agrarian nations need continuous water supply and effective drainage.'

You almost forgot to blink; his speech captivated you so. You made mental notes to ask someone about the meaning of the words you didn't understand, while cursing the previous ruler for not educating you well enough.

'The lands in the North and West were dry, while the East and South were fertile valleys with frequent rains. Many empires of the olden days benefited from building dams, waterways like aqueducts, and water-mills. These infrastructures can help us control and facilitate the distribution of water. The terrains of our Empire have the right geography for this plan to take place.'

These words, the wisest counsel you had ever received since becoming the Ruler, and they came from a street urchin!

'Second, our trading activities were erratic. There are too many mid-men, security and logistic issues, as well as difficulties obtaining supplies. These are all basics in trading. We build a warehouse, no, no, a marketplace, where people buy and sell goods in the open. The trade will flow smoother. Our farm produce, livestock, and carpentry can be distributed to the whole Empire. Starvation or scarcity shouldn't be an issue anymore.'

The three advisors and you were astonished. Who was this young man, and who taught him the intricacies of managing an empire?

'Thirdly, well, Sovereign Ruler, this third point may seem trivial, but do not underestimate its importance. We must distract the citizens. Distraction will snuff out any attempts to raise an opposition. They will never be able to garner enough support or maintain enough focus to generate resistance.'

'Keep going, keep going!' Now you were excited.

'I picture a giant amphitheatre, able to fit in thousands of people, like the Coliseum in the old civilization, where games and contests were played. Where people celebrated festivals and had feasts. Thus entertained, their sorrows would briefly leave them, they would forget to protest, their fury would soothe. They would even praise your wisdom and worship your legacy, Sovereign Ruler, because human beings treasure most what made them happy.'

The Great Hall was quiet for a very long time. Minutes stretched in silence, and the only sound was that of humans breathing and dry wind blowing from outside. The afternoon sun glided down the sky, pouring light from just the correct angle to frame the young man's figure in a mystical halo.

You rose and approached the young man, whose mind was absolutely more robust than his frail build. Your right hand gripped the golden sword by its hilt. You could see dark clouds crossing the brows of the three advisors, the governor, and the rows of guards—they were anticipating yet another bloodbath.

They did not expect you to embrace the young man like a father welcoming his long-lost son. Perhaps, if the previous ruler was more of a man, you would have missed him in that particular moment.

'Who are you, young man? O saviour, where have you been all this while? What took you so long to arrive to our doors, when we have suffered so hard?'

You glared at the three cowering advisors. They really were good at nothing other than cowering.

'Feed, clothe, and house this young man. O young man, o saviour, I want to hear so much more from you.'

Barely a week has passed when you began to notice differences. The Trades Advisor renovated the Empire warehouse into a huge marketplace. The desolate, dusty building regained life. New blocks were constructed, separating produce into type and condition. Certain walls that were getting in the way were demolished, providing more space and mobility. Soon, traders started to arrive in their caravans, carts, and beasts of burden, loaded with goods to sell, with hope in their hearts. There were plenty of raw produce such as paddy, corn, berries, animal hides, meat, fish, and livestock. People were also selling their handcrafted weapons, furniture, clothes, weavings, jewellery, and basic tools. The Empire regained its life. The people regained their hope to live.

'Who taught you all this?' You edged closer to the young man with every passing day. He was but a peasant's son in his late teens, whose lands were confiscated (probably by your decrees, but you'd rather not think of unpleasant things like that, not when the Empire was beginning to flourish and your foul mood was improving). His parents and siblings all died in poverty. His life was spared somehow, and he managed to reach the city. He didn't do much even in the city—like almost every other poor people from the villages, he begged for a living. Until he had the inspiration to offer his thoughts to the Sovereign Ruler.

'My father taught me. Before he died.' Of what, he was tactful enough not to mention.

'He taught me to read. Read history. Read stories on culture and technology. He has gone, but what I learnt stayed with me.'

'How much have you read?'

'Hundreds, maybe thousands of books,' he smiled, dimples showing. The sunken eyes and gaunt cheeks of the previous few months were gone, now that he was looking healthier and more substantial, you could see the charisma in his features.

He told his stories, teaching you about the books he read. How to manage the rise and fall of inflation, regulating currencies, banking, distribution of expenditures, this and that, and much more. The topics sometimes so perplexed you, but you made noble efforts to listen. To learn. He told you about history. How an empire soared and crashed. He said that every wisdom he had, he learnt from history.

'What was the most precious treasure history has ever recorded?' You asked him one day. He was silent for a while, and when he answered, he sounded hesitant.

'Black gold, Sovereign Ruler. Black gold was the most precious treasure in history, and it was the Black Gold that led to the destruction of the last human civilization.'

Greed seized you.

'Where can we find this Black Gold?'

'Our national treasury will surely benefit if we rediscovered the treasure. The greatest advantage will be enjoyed by our people, who are already tasting the fruits of progress.' You hastily added. You should at least make a show of concern for the welfare of your subjects, especially to this young man.

If he sensed the foul scent of your greed, he was wise enough not to show contempt. He wrote a series of instructions, drew several maps, and you clandestinely sent a convoy of your ten best warriors to find the treasure.

The Development Advisor was working hard building the dam, also following the young man's instructions. He designed it all—the layout, the blueprint, complete with algorithms and engineering technologies that had been forgotten since the last civilization died. The dam was the most intimidating behemoth of a structure, building it the most difficult endeavour. Prisoners and paid labourers toiled night and day, day and night. They carried stones, chopped and arranged logs. They dug tunnels and drilled holes. Valleys and paddy fields were padded with landfill.

The result was breathtaking. A civilizational milestone. Clean water filled drains and wells hundreds of miles to the north. Agriculture, animal husbandry, and domestic routines were fruitless drudges no more. The Empire was flourishing with prosperity, and you were at the head of it all as the glorious Ruler.

Another avant-garde suggestion was brought forth by the young man. You never doubted him—he was sent from heaven to illuminate your way to greatness. He proposed building schools, libraries, and universities. Human beings are *Homo discens. Homo educanus. Homo creator.* An empire, according to the young man, will thrive not only through the wisdom of rulers and aristocrats. He wanted to teach the people to read. Learned people will be the foundation of a great empire. You were immediately captivated by the idea. You immediately saw your role as the Sovereign Ruler in this. A Sovereign Ruler to a great Empire.

Tradition dictated that only three advisors were to exist at any particular moment. Uh, traditions could be altered. The Ruler's right hand can scratch away any decree and write new ones. You appointed the young man as the fourth advisor—the Education Advisor. Your action stunned the entire royal assembly, the entire Empire. Your action was drastic and earthshattering. Your action, not surprisingly, planted seeds of anger and resentment.

Your closeness with the young advisor made the three veteran advisors restless. All matters of the Empire were not discussed with them or brought to the royal assembly anymore. Four-eyes-discussions between you and the young advisor were enough to achieve satisfactory conclusions and conceive bright new ideas. Glares and whispers, and sideways glances haunted the palace halls and corridors, increasing in intensity each day.

The three idiot advisors visited you with increasing frequency, whispering ill about the young advisor. The young one was too ambitious, he was using the Ruler's genuine concern for the wellbeing of the people for his own advantage, the young advisor's intricate plans were bound to exhaust the Empire's resources and bring everything crashing down, et cetera, et cetera. You knew their dark desires only too well, and usually they only received hollered insults and disgraceful dismissals for their efforts. Nevertheless, the three advisors were persistent and crafty, and their slanders slowly needled their way into your suspicions.

'This new advisor is a very young man, Sovereign Ruler. Much younger than you, or the three of us old men. Imagine in ten years' time, where will he be, and where will you be. He is too clever for any of us, Sovereign Ruler. He is going to be always ahead, ten or twenty steps ahead of us. Please, Sovereign Ruler. Do not let his wiles deceive you.'

Those whispers left their marks upon your heart. And their whispers became louder, the marks deeper, as construction of the giant amphitheatre began. The Defence Advisor was given charge over the project. Located not far from the palace, originally an abandoned structure from the far-away past, thousands of manpower poured into transforming it to become an edifice of luxury.

Throughout the construction, you could hear how sweet the young advisor's name sounded by the lips of your subjects. How admirable, how clever, how revolutionary was this young man! He was no ordinary politician, and definitely not a lowly minion who existed to lick the bunions of your feet—this young man is an architect of civilization. Visionary. Genius. Deity incarnate. The superlatives eventually broke through the palace walls and changed your dreams into nightmares.

Several years passed and the amphitheatre was standing in all its glory. Finally, the long-awaited moment has arrived. The first ceremony to take place here would begin a new tradition for the Empire. You envisioned an extravagant, exotic festival. The workforce beneath you gave their all to make your vision happen, in the one month they had before the grand opening. Announcements were made to places far and near. Messengers from the new kingdom in the West were also invited, ostensibly as a diplomatic move. Your unspoken intent was clear: after witnessing the magnificence of the Empire, they would return to their lands, and think long and hard before ever conceiving any ill intention.

This is a wealthy Empire. Plentiful. Strong. Modern. Spearheading civilization. *Homo historicus*. An empire that is winning, and is going to conquer. You were the Sovereign Ruler, and the first page of history would testify to that!

The celebrations took seven days and seven nights. Mornings, noons, and nights, subjects competed in all sorts of contests. The winners received hurrahs and gifts, and women; those who didn't win weren't particularly dejected either, as they were mostly drunken in revelry. Food and drinks overflowed, filling the bellies of humans and animals alike, that both kinds were seen vomiting and defecating by the streets. Citizens of the Empire were totally stoned, inebriated with entertainment. You had it all figured out. Planned meticulously to the last detail—the final moment, on the seventh day, before the festival concluded—when you rose from your seat of honour, lifting your sword of gold, and made a royal proclamation. Your voice boomed like a decree from the heavens.

'There is a traitor among us. A wolf in sheep's clothing, standing hidden biding his time until he saw the opportunity to bring the Empire down. He came begging for mercy, thus was fed and clothed, given security against all threats. We gave him a grand title, a glorified position by my side. We gave him honour and dignity. But what did he give us in return? How did he show gratitude? He bit the hand that fed him. He spat on the bowl that he drank from. He wanted to rob the Empire of its wealth. The wealth our people gathered with our sweat and blood!'

The amphitheatre was wrapped in silence, the subjects pausing their celebrations to listen. Advisors, governors, and royalties were trying not to stare at each other in bewilderment.

You unsheathed your sword against the young advisor's neck, who was sitting on your right hand's side, just as bewildered as the others. His eyes widened in terror and comprehension, as he understood what was being done.

'Guards, arrest this deceitful young advisor! Shackle him in the deepest dungeons!' Everything happened so fast. No one had seen this coming. The public spectators stared in amazement and confusion, seeing the young advisor manhandled and roughly dragged out by the guards.

Why? What was his crime?

As if on cue, drums, flutes, and guitars immediately started an intoxicating beat. Dancers jumped onstage, gyrating their bodies to the rhythm, and they were quickly joined by the subjects. All too ready to forget that anything out of ordinary has ever happened.

The young advisor's name was smeared and then erased.

While the people, the *Homo ludens*, were partying their heads and consciences away.

After Time 5: The Scholar II

'IMPOSSIBLE! That couldn't be true!' You exclaimed in disbelief. 'How old are you now?'

'Twenty,' the voice was feeble, drained of vigour.

'So, you became the Young Advisor at the age of seventeen?' You still found it hard to believe, yet rather exciting. An interesting morsel to add some thrill to your monotonous life in the dungeons.

For three days and three nights you leaned with your ear against the wall, straining to hear any sounds made by your next-cell neighbour. There wasn't much else to do there. His young voice, almost boyish, was tell-tale for his youthfulness. You had been an occupant of these dark cells for almost ten years, give or take. You weren't too sure; it wasn't like you had a calendar here.

Throughout those years you've met all sorts of characters, heard plenty of tales—some more bizarre than the others. Dungeon cells were some sort of an alphabet soup, where various individuals from odd walks of life were thrown together. You were no stranger to strangeness. Yet, this new inmate was different. His stories were unusually intricate, with complex plots and hyperbolic concepts you struggled to understand. His words were finely sculpted and delicately put together, riddled with aesthetic symbolisms and confusing metaphors.

Other prisoners you had met—while waiting for their sentences—they would talk of revolution, their righteous anger, desire for revenge, and how they were betrayed. They would talk about subversive plans to overthrow the Ruler. In the dark, they spoke about poverty, cruelty, robberies, fires and murders, and every other dollop of blackness that stained their lives. They lived cursed lives, rot in their souls spreading to their physical bodies. Their disenchantment poisoned their wills to live—and most of them only wished for death, the quicker the better, and hopefully not too painful.

This new next-cell neighbour, this new 'friend', was different from the rest.

He had a humble beginning. Youngest-born in a farming family, with an elder sister, three elder brothers, a loving mother, and a caring father. They lived in a shabby hut, put together from sticks and clumps of straw. Their small farm produced enough bananas and wheat to feed the family. However, one day a horde of soldiers came to demand part of the produce for themselves. These soldiers, more appropriately called bandits, did the same to many other families in the area. They came almost every month, demanding more and more food to fill their sacks. The farmers ran out of food even to feed themselves. Frustrated in their demands, the soldier-bandits went berserk, burning houses and seizing lands. Your neighbour's family suffered the same fate, and they had to escape to the forest with only the clothes on their backs.

Every single member of his family dead, leaving him alone, your neighbour crawled his way to the city. One day he went to the palace and was immediately accepted by the Sovereign Ruler. This was where the story turned strange. He was adopted by the Ruler, treated almost like a son, taught the Ruler himself many things, even bestowed the robes of an Empire Advisor.

'So you were behind the construction of the marketplace and the famous dam?'

'I merely gave suggestions,' your new neighbours, ever gentle and humble.

'What about the giant amphitheatre that sent its drumbeats to the edges of the city, even audible down here in these dungeons?'

'Same, I gave suggestions. Ironically, I was the sacrifice in its first show.' You heard disturbing tones in the final sentence. Having communicated by listening only for the past ten years, you were a master in detecting inflections and tonal nuances in speech. This young man wasn't giving you good vibes.

The other side of the wall was silent afterwards, only punctuated by occasional bouts of heavy breathing. Perhaps the man was tired, or sleeping, or was communicating with his silence. His words meant so much, his silence must be meaningful too. For the next three days, no conversations took place between the two of you. Your eavesdropping revealed nothing extraordinary—you heard coughs and sighs, your neighbour's footsteps pacing the narrow cell, his chewing that sounded so loud in the quiet emptiness, his snores. He was only different from you and the rest of the inmates when he spoke his mind. You knew there must be one thing that he knew, that was how he set himself apart.

'Teach me to read,' he did not respond immediately to your request, but you knew he was listening.

'Teach me to read,' you repeated. He remained quiet. You repeated the request, again and again, all day long. He responded with the impenetrable silence, until you almost gave up and told yourself that this might just be one more prisoner who had lost his hope, no different from the rest.

That night, when the guard came to distribute food for dinner, you heard his voice.

'Give my food to the person in the next cell.'

That was unexpected and incomprehensible. The guard obeyed without much fuss. Probably he still had some vestiges of respect for the supposedly noble prisoner. Probably he just didn't want to waste his energy with aggression.

The plate slid under your trapdoor. You opened the banana leaf that covered it. It was the usual fare—rice and pieces of nuts—but arranged into unfamiliar lines.

'Follow my pronunciation, and copy the lines on the cell wall,' he whispered. Wasting no time, you reached for a rock and began scratching similarly shaped lines on your cell wall.

That was how you begun. He taught you reading using letters written with grains of rice and nuts on a plate. You copied and repeated the pronunciations like a parrot. A dutiful, diligent parrot, who learned the letters every day, all day, memorizing them. Once you learned the letters, your neighbour taught you how to form syllables. Then you constructed words, developed phrases, and before too long, you could write simple sentences. It was mystical, almost magical, how your mind expanded so wide within the confines of a stifling cell.

Your neighbour was normally a man of few words, but when he felt like it, he would tell stories. When he didn't feel like talking, he would be silent, sometimes his silence stretched for days. Every time you heard his voice you would be immediately alerted, you would rise from wherever you were crouching and went to lean your ear against the part of the wall where you could hear him best, and listened with undivided focus.

Time flew so fast when you were listening to the sage in the cell.

He would talk about books he had read. He shared his philosophies for an ideal empire. Social hierarchy. Cultures. Ethos. Civilization. Development. Technology. He scattered jargons here and there, but his stories always flowed smoothly like water. His head was like a repository of knowledge, once contained in books, now residing in his mind.

'It didn't surprise me that the Ruler feared your wisdom so much,' you blurted out once, and as payback for your slip of tongue, you got a week's silence. He was quiet. He did not teach you to read. You were chastised and vowed to better watch your mouth.

One morning, you heard noises coming from the outside world. To reach the dungeons, the noises must be very loud, you wondered what could cause them. You heard prison doors clanging open and banged shut, you heard screams and fights among the newer inmates that were apparently being thrown into the dungeon in droves.

'What happened, guard?' curiosity squeezed words out of your next-cell neighbour.

'New order from the Sovereign Ruler,' the guard answered, sounding reluctant. He didn't want to be perceived as fraternizing with the prisoners. There were more guards in the dungeons now, his actions could be seen by scheming eyes. Corruption and double-crossing existed at every level.

'What do you mean?'

'They were closing schools and libraries. Some were burned,' the guard answered, in a low voice. He glanced around, making sure no one was watching. 'The people were no longer allowed to read, to teach, or to learn reading. Books were taken from houses and burned. Books were thrown into the river, some said the water turned black from the dissolved ink.'

'But . . . why?'

The guard, despite all his precautions, was keen to share the gossip.

'Apparently, the palace declared royal proprietary upon all forms of writing. Only the noblemen and the Ruler himself are allowed to read. Teachers who taught reading were arrested and imprisoned, charged with treason. Within a week they will all be sentenced.'

The news was shocking, and your next-cell neighbour must have felt the blow much harder. He founded schools and libraries in the empire. He taught the empire to read.

'What was the sentence going to be?' You took your turn asking, because your neighbour had fallen silent.

'I heard that a ship was being built. The convicts would be crammed onto the ship and left adrift in the open sea, with no food or drinks. They would be left to die of hunger and dehydration, piled on top of each other under the sun.'

You joined your neighbour's silence. You vowed to hide this new skill you had. This knowledge kills, merely knowing how to read and write could turn you into carcass for seagull food. You still wanted to live, thank you very much, although for the time being your existence was limited by the roof and walls of your cell. You were the eternal optimist. Meanwhile outside, chaos still ruled, you heard screams and indeterminate noises— some heart-rending, some frightening. You counted, it was almost five days before the dungeon regained its usual quiet.

One day, the guard slid you a plate from the next cell. You were excited, the previous plate was quite a while ago. Underneath the banana leaf covering, the grains were arranged in an unusual pattern. You knew the images were not letters, but something else. Strange shapes.

'Copy it to the wall. Memorize it.'

You shut your mouth and obeyed. You didn't want to say something wrong and offend your neighbour into another long silence. Ten years in the dungeon wasn't very conducive to build your social skills.

Almost every day, a plate would arrive under your trap door, containing another chunk of pattern. You would copy the pattern, connect it to the main picture on your wall that was steadily growing bigger, and attempt to memorize the image. The true shape was slowly emerging—that of a map.

'I have read the prophecies,' he suddenly spoke, when you were staring at the picture on your wall, now looking complete. There was not much else to do, so anything that took your mind off the monotony of day-to-day existence was welcome, even if it was just drawing and memorizing an irrelevant picture. For could there be anything less relevant to an incarcerated prisoner who may never see the light of the day, than a map?

'In the Ruler's palace there was an abandoned old chamber. No one opened it—but I did. There were archived Empire documents inside— some were important, some were not. I found several that I was sure would be classified secret, but in our time, nobody actually cares enough for written documents. If they read it, they would learn the history of the Empire since its birth. They would learn about the first ruler, the Red-Headed Ruler.'

You eased yourself into your regular position, leaning against the wall to listen.

'During the reign of the second ruler, there was a wise blind man. He had visions, or dreams, of the past and the future,' you could hear how difficult it was for the words to come out. Your next-cell neighbour was a young man, but he sounded old. Old and ill. 'He prophesied the future of the Empire. He saw the dam and the amphitheatre being built. The Empire prospering and progressing. Nevertheless, he also saw the Empire's destruction. He saw a ruler who destroyed books and a people who no longer read. He saw the vicious fights over who got to walk in the corridors of power. He saw the dam abandoned and unmaintained.'

You kept your ears open.

'You, my neighbour, will walk out of this prison. The map on your wall showed the way to a building, way at the outskirts of the Empire. In the building, I stored books. I made notes of very useful things and kept it there, too. Bring everything to the new kingdom in the west.

The people had white hair, and their bodies were sturdier than us. Find their king, and teach them to read. Teach them all to read.'

'You spoke a lot of nonsense, dear pal, but this made the least sense of all. I have been imprisoned for ten years. They have forgotten about me. I will never be free.'

Your request to learn reading, your enthusiasm to listen to his tales, were all ways for you to distract yourself, to make life bearable, to preserve your sanity. You might not have any expectation to be free, but you still had the will to survive.

'I have arranged it. You will walk out of this place after I die.'

Die?

Before you could babble about how reprehensible it would be to wait eagerly for one's friend to die while anticipating freedom, he spoke further, now in a voice so weak it was barely a whisper. You glued your ear to the wall, catching and memorizing every word. Sometimes you scratched a note on the wall. It was a long message with complicated schemes, and you felt yourself getting anxious.

'If this failed, I will lose my head,' you grumbled. You did not want to die. But without taking the risk, you would never live for real.

That was the last time you heard his voice—the young advisor who was too smart for his own safety. He starved to death in his cell. A commotion rose among the guards. High officials came to witness his corpse carried out. That was the first time you saw him—peering from the bars of your cell—his emaciated, small body. Skin and bone. No muscles, no hair. He was malnourished. You immediately thought of all those plates of food that he never ate, but passed next door to teach you. Guilt consumed you. Loss overcame you. For the first time since you were locked behind the bars, you wept.

As predicted, the Ruler summoned you to the palace hall. After ten years, you recoiled at the glare of sunlight, then gradually welcomed it. A delicious pain. You heard birdsong, sniffed the cool scent of trees, and enjoyed the gentle heat of the day. As predicted by your late neighbour.

'What did your neighbour tell you in prison?' the Sovereign Ruler broke your reverie with his harsh bark.

'Not much. He was very quiet,' you gave him the pre-planned answer.

'There must be something. Don't you dare lie to me!' you marvelled inside at what a short-tempered man this ruler was. He had no control over his greed.

'He told me something about Black Gold.'

Like a monkey offered a banana, the Ruler's eyes lit up. His expression softened immediately.

'That's it. Go on!'

'Black gold was a precious ore from the previous civilization. People fought over it and wars broke because of the fights. That was why they destroyed each other.'

'Do you know where the Black Gold was hidden?'

You remained silent, as if deep in thought.

'Where was the Black Gold hidden?' the Ruler repeated his question in a harsher tone.

'Yes, yes, I can tell you, Sovereign Ruler. But I wanted something in exchange.'

'Whatever you wanted,' the Ruler answered instantly. Your late neighbour was right, this ruler was predictable and playable. No wonder he was so easily tricked to dispose of such an intelligent asset like the young advisor.

'I have been incarcerated for ten years, forgotten and ignored, given no trials. I want my freedom.'

The Ruler sat on his throne, looking smug and powerful. He grinned and laughed, greed eminent on his expression. He stroked his ceremonial sword, adorned with Black Gold. Three advisors on his side conferred among themselves. Whispers arose from everyone in the hall, filling the air of the seemingly quiet hall with a soft murmur.

'Fine. Today onwards, you are a free man!'

You smiled, then you wept. Your shoulders shook, tears and snot streamed on your face. You thought of the lifeless body of your fellow inmate, his tortured and ill shell dragged out by the guard. First, he was your teacher. Now, you owed him your life.

You requested for coal and a piece of wood you could draw on, and scratched an image of a map you had memorized. The Ruler could not stop guffawing, as he watched your drawing, his eyes full of lust. Greed and lust made people so easy to manipulate, you thought.

After you satisfied the Ruler, as promised, you walked out into the world. No one saw any importance in preventing a lowly ex-prisoner like you from leaving. Even if you knew the map, you would never have enough brains or power to look for the Black Gold yourself. That must be what the Ruler and his noblemen thought. They did not know that you had another trail to follow.

They did not know that you had a promise to honour.

After Time 6: Amputation

I placed my ears against your chest, I could hear your heart rebelling. Your malnourished figure, lying sprawled like a carcass grilled by the sun, was not going to last much longer.

'We must do it.'

'Impossible,' your voice was weak, you have been repeating similar nonsensical things, you were delirious.

You have been discarded from life for too long. Fifty-eight scratches on the bark of the coconut tree, marking the passage of time since you landed here—fifty-eight days until the past few days when you were finally forced to admit defeat—too weak to stand, to move, or to count days.

'We must do it, if we want to live,' I whispered, and you hallucinated. 'This is a punishment, your sins coming to haunt you. This is the time for us to purify ourselves. To reincarnate as a new man,' you stared at me. And shivered.

Yes, you told me everything in your delirium. Let me repeat your story. It begun with how you were betrayed, left adrift in a floating raft, only armed with a single knife. Your right-hand man was bought by a political foe. When the sedative wore off, you were no longer in the banquet. You were on a raft, floating in the middle of nowhere. But they forgot that this is your territory. Threats to survival were clay in your hands—you were manipulative, exploitive, crafty, a hunter. Those were your identity, the red in your blood. *Homo venator*, aren't you?

Sorry, you're too comical, you made me laugh too hard. Please stop the heroic act.

We are not going to die here so easily, said you, while pointing to a bird carcass not far from where you laid. That was our breakfast a few days ago, did you still remember? Did you still remember how did you survive in the beginning? First, you built a shelter. This island is as just as big as a field. Several coconut palms were scattered here and there, like misplaced goalposts. You took the fronds and bound them with fibrous twine from the palm leaves. You gathered the coconuts and dug the roots, trying to stave off hunger. Little by little. But they did not last very long—you finally ran out. With the one knife you have, you started chasing crabs and small fish on the shores. You clung to life so hard.

'That was before. Now, you were just a fragile dehydrated body, all the survival drained out of you.'

For a while, you were still holding your life. Survival was your game, and you were playing it well—until that disastrous night. After the fifty-eighth scratch on the coconut tree, a monstrous storm hit the island, and the sea shook with an ungodly violence. The small island quaked like a floating log in the waves. The storm extinguished the moon, and the night was so dark you were a blind man groping for exit in a boiling pan. There was nothing left in the next day—all resource for life was washed away by the storm. Except for a knife. You. And a beached seagull broken by the storm just like you, dragging its broken wings and cracked leg bones on the drying sand. You sank into depression, and I came in your head as a hallucinatory companion.

'I have sharpened this knife a few days ago. It is still sharp. Take it, get a good grip, and make your choice,' I had told you.

You stared at the seagull every day, limping and struggling, two-arms wide from where you laid motionless. You wondered if the seagull was also staring at you. Perhaps the two of you were silently competing— who would die first? Both of you were struggling with hunger. You could only drag your limbs in pain, both your legs in paresis, semi-paralysed after the storm. In your eyes, the bird was a hot roasted meal, taunting you to just move forward an inch, then another inch . . . you salivated at the sight, at the thought, but your body wouldn't cooperate.

Then, the bird showed you its determination to survive.

It began pecking at its useless, broken wing. Strand by strand, it pulled out its feathers, exposing pale brown skin. Then it pecked again.

With its sharp beak, the bird pulled at its own skin, tearing it off. Sometimes it let out a shrill cry of pain, then after a while the bird continued doggedly ripping its skin. Blood oozed, but didn't gush out. You stared. Sweet pink flesh was exposed. The seagull began to devour its own flesh—hunger has triumphed over pain. The bird ate one of its wings; ate the flesh to the bone, as far as it could reach.

'The bird was teaching you.'

'But that was just a bird! An animal.'

'Nature is the best teacher for survival. We were *Homo imitans*. In one of the old civilizations, birds taught humans how to bury our dead. Did you not remember the tale?'

You laughed, a soundless laughter, but I knew how loud it was. The laughter offended me. How arrogant of you! You said that destiny never determined your fate; you always wrote your own. I knew, I knew. I heard it from you a million times. You started from a filthy, degenerate place, uncharted on any maps. You said that you were thrown there by a conspiracy between destiny and the universe, together they decided that you were to be born from a nameless woman's womb, born to belong to no one, meant to own nothing. But that was the first and the last time you allowed those conspirators to win over you. You crawled and climbed up the ladders of survival, pushing all other equally greedy competitors to fall flat on their ugly faces. The last thing you remembered, the number one place in the Empire was mere inches from your reach, before you found yourself thrown first onto the sands of this forsaken island.

'Take this knife, hold it tight. Choose the most useless and sinful part of your body. Amputate it. We will eat it together. We need to live!' I hardened my voice, like a commander's, and you began to shiver again.

You opened your eyes. Your lips were dried and bruised. Your skin was flaking into reddish-white lesion. Clumps of your hair were missing, leaving bald patches crusty with dandruff. Glints of the merciless sun reflected off the tip of the blade, catching your eyes. Drying pieces of seagull bones were scattered next to it. With all your will, you hauled your weighty body towards the knife, reaching for it with an increasingly trembling hand. You were becoming encephalopathic, toxins gathering in your body from the prolonged period of starvation and malnutrition were invading your brain.

'Alright. This leg is too sinful. This leg,' you touched the cool blade against your left leg. Ready to slice. Hunger was clenching its sharp teeth against your belly.

Your adolescence was stained and putrid. You hated the two-storey, rundown garage where you and the other thirteen kids took shelter. All of you were homeless kids—young children and slightly older teenagers, all orphaned, with dead or missing parents. As the oldest kid, you were their leader. Being 'big brother' to a pack of street rats was too sentimental an endeavour. It killed your potential.

You had to worry about feeding them. Keeping their tummies full was important, so they wouldn't cry and whine all night long. You were all beggars, and you had to beg not only for yourself, but for all these kids you bear no relation to. You were exhausted and wanted out. This situation had trapped you like a hamster on a wheel, the faster you ran, the faster the wheel turned—but you remained in the exact same spot.

The opportunity arrived one night when everybody was fast asleep. The dying fire in the hearth downstairs spread to the floorboards and caught the window drapes. You and thirteen of your brothers (there is no need to feign guilt; they are no blood relation of yours!) were trapped in the second floor. It was then that you saw it—the exit door to release you from the chains that kept you bound for years. A skylight window, opened on the slanting roof, with a ladder leading to it. You wasted no time and climbed up, your way to freedom.

You looked behind and your brothers were trying to follow suit. Struggling with the heat, coughing in the smoke, trying to catch hold on the wooden rungs with hands slippery with sweat. To doubt is cowardice, you whispered, and kicked the ladder with your left leg once you're safely out on the roof.

For an eternal second, the ladder wobbled, before sliding and falling into the thick burning smoke, carrying on it three or four of your 'brothers'. They fell straight into the gaping mouth of fire, their screams quickly muffled by their chokes. You walked away without turning back, not even once. You had no need of nightmares, or memories of their crying and screaming. Good night, prison; good morning, freedom! You began your new day as a free man—with your left foot forward.

'Hold on.' Your hand, ready to slice the left leg, suddenly stopped in its motions. 'This leg is not the most damned, right? It has its share of goodness. It brought me out of the dark alleys, leading the first steps. I shouldn't dispose of it so easily.'

'Hey. Faster, please! Don't dawdle!' I fretted. I was angry. I was hungry!

Still with a trembling hand, you brought the blade against your left arm. You nicked the skin, a small cut—but no blood came out. Perhaps you're too dehydrated; the blood was all but dried up.

'Yes. Yes. This left hand might be the most damned.' You mumbled, your cracked larynx barely producing an audible voice.

'No doubting, please. This is no game.' I pleaded, encouraged, trying to hide my disgust at your lack of fortitude. You then laughed again in your mind—of course I could see it, and it disgusted me further, and reminisced about the stupid drunk politician who once was affectionate towards you.

'He loved me.'

You told me so many times about him. You started as a lowly errand boy to a lowly player in politics. The story of your miraculous escape—sole survivor of a garage fire that took the lives of thirteen street urchins—became the talk of the town. The old chap took pity on you—no, rather, he took advantage of the situation, and invited you to stay with him. The gesture would gain him a little bit of publicity and reputation as a good samaritan.

He was a lonely man. His wife and children left him because he regarded them as little more than trophies, decorations to display in a mansion on a hill. He was your first mentor, showing you the stairs to the top and teaching you the first steps to get there. At night he would get drunk and mutter in slurred speech about desires, cunning, scandals, envy, grudges, betrayals, and conspiracies. The political jargons popped up so often and planted seeds in your opportunistic head.

For the first time, you saw the world as a big chessboard, and you wanted to choose your position in it. First, you were not going to be a pawn. You were sure of it. You were sure that your exit from the world of beggars, and your subsequent entrance into this mansion was no coincidence.

You inched closer to the lonely politician. He had won the governor's trust somehow, and granted a small piece of territory to earn from. Your position crept upwards—from an errand boy to an advisor-companion. In his eyes, you're like a son (or a sounding-board?). Every time he told you about the ups and downs of his life or cursed his political enemies, you listened attentively without any words. You learned to project the façade of utmost loyalty while cultivating your inner opportunist—until the decrepit politician whispered your name to the governor as his successor.

He forgot his own lesson, the old man. Do not trust anyone but your own self.

He gave the sword too soon to you—the sword that would eventually slice his own neck off.

One evening, as the politician was riding his favourite mount, you executed your plans. A favourite pastime among the local elites, to ride the horse-like beast to the top of a hill, then speed downwards while avoiding strategically placed obstacles. Your left hand, the damned left hand, was the one responsible to fit the saddle. It wasn't difficult to loosen the ropes a little bit. Then you sat aside and watched.

The old man broke his osteoporotic spine. He became paralyzed, from the neck downwards. A bed for him to live his last days, a mansion for you!

'This left hand opened the mansion door for me.' You stopped slicing. 'No, no, we mustn't eat it yet, my left hand has done me a lot of good.'

'So let us just die of hunger then,' I sulked. And you merely laughed. How annoying.

'Come on, don't lose your temper yet. This, this right leg might be the most useless part of my body. The most sinful. Here, look, I'm cutting it.'

You pressed the glistening blade against your right leg. Tried to angle the sharp edge to cut, but your hand slipped. You tried again, but your hand shook too hard, and the blade brushed against your inflamed skin without drawing any blood.

Damn! I waited with a pounding heart. Anxious, if you were really going to make it or not.

You were a visionary. *Homo ambitious.* Big and voracious appetite—I mean ambition. Blessed with a sugary tongue. As the appointed successor for the bedbound old politician, the governor was quickly taken with you. In his words, you had a complete package to be a politician. Good looks, eloquent, elegant, high taste, intelligent, and composed. You would listen respectfully, while complimenting the governor and telling him that you still had a long way to go with someone like him to aspire to. Meanwhile, behind his back, you would laugh your head off when thinking of the potbellied governor giving his so-called 'charismatic' speeches.

After several short months the governor trusted you with several warehouses and bazaar sites. You were given important positions. Once a month, you accompanied him to present the revenue of your region to the Sovereign Ruler in the capital of the Empire. You never wasted any opportunity—you caught the Ruler's eyes as easily as you had the governor's and the old politician. It was just as easy to convince the Ruler that you were the future—charismatic and idealistic, while the governor is just an old mount who was neither fast nor mobile anymore.

The governor was initially a stepping stone; then he became an obstacle rock. You must kick the rock off the road, so you can travel forwards and upwards as you had always wanted. As the two of you were traveling home to your region, after another audience with the Ruler, the governor regaled you again with his black and corrupted stories. The same tales you have heard from the old man. You couldn't wait to dispose of this boring old codger.

It was quick and clean. No mess. You were my second mentor, and you have done an excellent service—your last words before your right leg kicked his ample butt, sending him down a deep ravine. He rolled like the rock you saw him as—with not a squeak nor a scream. The governor was gone, missing, no news of him at all. You cooked up a story of how he was missing during your travel, how you had tried your best to look for him, how sad you were for having lost a great mentor. Easy. Too easy.

'Wait, wait,' for the third time, your hand was stilled. Black-red blood was finally oozing from the leg. Why must you stop? You're so exasperating!

'This right leg has kicked away all the obstacles, clearing the road so I could walk towards victory.'

'So?' I am beyond bored.

'So, it was not useless. Sinful, perhaps. But not useless. This right leg has proven its value.'

You actually opened your mouth and tried to produce a believable laugh. Not much came out but stink from your rotten teeth and your acidotic breath, courtesy of your failing liver and kidneys.

'If that was so, then we can just cut off the right hand. Stop dilly-dallying, would you?' I was tired of your guiles. Wait, wasn't guiles and twisting tongues part of your game? You were keen to keep at it, even when your life was at the end of its tethers.

The blade changed hands—not from yours to mine, but from the right hand to the left. You were hesitant. You looked at me for conviction.

'Come on, we need to eat,' I encouraged.

The Sovereign Ruler had three main advisors. Underneath them, there were three governors (one of them was the potbellied one, currently resting in peace in the bottom of some desolate ravine). Further under them, there were twelve chiefs (one of them was the paralyzed old politician, in his bed waiting for the mercy of death to let him rest). The pyramid of power was a tradition, you weren't totally sure started by whom. *Homo hierarchicus*. Supposedly to guard the nobility of rulers and purity of blood, whatever those tosh means. Climbing the pyramid, from bottom to the top, was only possible when a vacancy existed—such as when an aristocrat died without a successor, paralyzed after a riding accident, or rolled down a ravine like a rock (you laughed again! Where was the joke, I wonder!)

You became the most juvenile governor in your time, perhaps in history. Disgust and envy sparked by that was phenomenal. Each of the three advisors kept a metaphorical blade of treason inside their robes, always ready to stab an exposed back. They believed that you were young, immature, too ambitious, too greedy.

Your youthfulness and perhaps, the well-known hatred surrounding you, rendered you the Ruler's favourite governor. 'Looking at you was like looking into a mirror,' said the Ruler. Those words shook and squeezed the hearts of every single advisor and governor in the audience.

They were like fish out of water, struggling for breath, suffocating in their spite. They knew that those words meant one thing—the Ruler was looking for his successor. Successor for the throne.

You knew that you were being watched. Your words, your actions, all became subject of scrutiny. Many eyes were looking for loopholes that could eventually be used to garrotte your neck. Some secret conspiracy was being concocted by the three advisors. You could feel their cold stares and cold hearts every time you were in the royal audience.

But your heart was colder.

The Ruler had a beautiful daughter, lusted upon by the men of the city. One of the advisors dared to fall in love in her, and she responded in kind. Clandestinely, they started an affair. They met under the cover of the night, exchanging warm embraces and words of yearning. Perhaps the night failed to weave a good cover, or the advisor was so passionate that he missed his footing—he was caught.

It was wrong for an aristocrat to desire, let alone romance, a ruler's daughter. The advisor was brought before the Ruler in chains. The Ruler was all but ready for sentencing—but the rule of court, apart from stating that romancing a princess was wrong, also stated that a clear witness was necessary before penalty can be passed. No one came forward. These nobles were perhaps remembering their own sins that the unfortunate advisor was covering, or maybe they recognized the sanctity of love. Neither qualm bothered your conscience. You crawled forward, raised your right hand, and swore the truth of your testimony.

You lied without remorse.

The advisor and the princess often met in the palace gardens, sometimes in the unused chambers or empty meeting rooms. You even saw them going into the forest once. You saw them do the unspeakable, the dishonourable. Perhaps if he wasn't so incensed by the extra bits in your false witness, the Ruler would have given a more merciful punishment, like a swift beheading. But in the Ruler's wrath, the advisor was sentenced to be tortured to death. He was tied to a riding beast, dragged up and down a hill, through paths littered by sharp rocks. After three such rounds, he wasn't screaming or breathing anymore, and his carcass was thrown to the forest for scavengers to feast on.

So, who would climb another step up the pyramid of power, taking the place of the dead advisor?

The answer was obvious.

'Wait! No! This right hand was not totally useless. It was my false testimony that brought me to the second most important place in the Empire! I must not destroy this right hand.' You stopped cutting. You opened and closed your right fist multiple times, admiring your own anatomy.

'Then, what are we going to eat?' I was despairing. This was hopeless. You were a hopeless case. 'If you die, your whole body would become useless anyway. So you better decide quick.'

You were silent for a long time. You stared at me as if I were a stranger. You seemed to not remember that throughout your life, I was your conscience, the voice inside your head that kept you surviving and breathing, bringing you from the filthy streets to the Empire's number two seat.

I was your survival instinct. Your hunger. Your lust!

And when I give orders, you must obey.

'Not the left leg. Not the left hand. Not the right leg. Not the right hand.' You stopped. You were floating in and out of delirium, barely holding thoughts and words together. 'There was only one thing that I truly hated in my body.'

'What?'

With a shaky left hand, you held the knife, lifted it higher, past your face, approaching the right earlobe. You slashed at it until it came off. Your lips were locked, you did not let out even a whimper. But your eyes were shut tight in pain.

Your right earlobe dropped on the sands, red and wet. The fresh wound where the appendage was once attached was also red and wet.

'This is our breakfast today,' you said, in a voice with almost no vigour. 'This ear is the bane of my existence. From now on, I want to hear no more sermons or persuasions from no one, not even you!'

I grinned and licked my lips. My tummy was growling. *Bon appetit* o my friend, o crafty survival warrior!

After Time 7: Cerberus

TRUE, that was its moniker. A fierce and mythical name. Greek mythology would have attached the name to an image of a shadowy beast from Hades, guardian of the gate of Hell. A crossbreed of two antagonistic creatures—Echidna, the beauty with a snake's body, and the giant Typhos with fingers that belong to a dragon. The name struck fear into the hearts of mortals and immortals alike, terrifying humans and spirits and even the deities who were supposedly safe in Olympus. Having the tail of a snake and the claws of a lion, the carnivore would pounce on any intruder who dared breach the underground inferno.

When you were young, you were one of the brave kids who laughed at the story. You said that only babies can be scared by bedtime tales.

Yet, time after time, when history has been erased and written over, anything was possible. Nuclear wars catalyzed mutations and evolutions (you would rather call them radiation damages). Of animals and plants. Humans, not exempted. When you saw the three-headed monster called *Cerberus*, you knew it was no mystical canine who once fought Hercules. It might look vicious, but it was a victim of humankind's viciousness.

Prior to its capture almost twenty years ago, *Cerberus* went on a rampage in a village by the edge of the Empire. The thing gorged on eight people, eating them alive to satisfy its hunger. Its body was four times the size of a sturdy horse. The three wolf-like heads were exceedingly ugly and horrifying, reddish drool dribbling from the edges of its mouths. Its manes were black and coarse, the leg muscles strong and prominent. The *Cerberus* howled like thunder, shaking earth and sky. When the humans managed to surround and entrap the monster, it fell into a deep valley gorge, badly injured. It woke up from a coma to find its four feet bound and each of its necks collared with a tight golden band. The *Cerberus* became the Empire trophy. A symbol of its strength and power. Images of it were incorporated as an emblem in flags, battle standards, even the palace curtains. From the most violent predator, its status was elevated to become a dignified royal icon.

'Although this monster has three heads, it only has one stomach. One excretory organ, too. Feeding one head is enough to keep all three satisfied and full,' explained the caretaker of *Cerberus*, a wiry small-built man with prominent scars, probably courtesy of the beast's claws. Throughout twenty years of its stay in the dank and dirty palace basement, the man has been the sole caretaker of the Ruler's favourite pet.

'What if you fed two or all three heads at once?'

'That is gluttony, and the *Cerberus* may choke itself to death,' the caretaker answered. 'Each of its head has a different age. The right head is the oldest, while the left is the youngest—like three brothers. According to the lore, each head could see three different ages—past, present, and future. That was why the Ruler named each of the heads after each of the three royal princes.'

'You still believe that?' you jeered with a chuckle. The left head of the *Cerberus* glared at you. The head was named Ta, after you, the youngest son of the Ruler. 'He must have seen my future on the throne. Don't you worry, *Cerberus*, when that time arrived you shall be my favourite pet dog, nuzzling against my legs.' You were still chuckling.

Today is the seventieth birthday of the Ruler. A descendant of the Red-Headed Ruler, who founded the Empire ten generations ago. The Ruler was old and frail, but friends and foes alike still expressed their admiration towards his leadership. The Empire under his reign was prosperous and peaceful. In honour of his seventieth birthday, for the first time ever, a tournament of sorts was held between his three sons. The official reason, stated by the Ruler, was nothing more than a test to let his sons prove their talent and mettle, as well as entertaining his good subjects. Yet those who could read between the lines realized that any old king needed a successor, and this tournament would determine which of the three princes would sit next on the throne.

The three princes, each known as one of the best warriors in the whole Empire, definitely did not regard the tournament as mere games. They were going to fight to death for their greatest desire.

Following a festive opening to the celebration, the three princes were escorted into the auditorium, attired in their warrior finest, riding their best, toughest-looking mounts. A product of evolution, the horse-like creatures were twice the size of normal mounts. Drums pounded with rhythms of battle and war. Citizens of the Empire filled the huge amphitheatre, screaming, cheering, throwing flowers and fragrant tokens. The display of grandeur was intoxicating. The Ruler stood and gave a salutary speech. The golden cup, one of the sacred symbols of the Empire, remained firmly in his hand. He was old, but his hands never trembled. His subjects cheered after him, enraptured by his magnetism.

The first prince was named Ra. The same name for the first, supposedly eldest head of the *Cerberus*. He was the most skilful rider the Empire had ever known, never defeated by any aspiring warriors. The first event in this tournament would be his biggest opportunity to shine. The three princes, Ra, Sa, and you, Ta, must ride their mounts of choice from the middle of the amphitheatre, directly to the edge of the city, and ride to the peak of Fire Mountain. The latent volcano has been standing there like a sleeping dragon since the beginning of the Empire's memory. The road to the top was steep, jutted with sharp rocks, and dotted with spurts of boiling geyser. Poisonous sulphur-tinged dust scattered in the air, blown everywhere by the wind. The mountain is a fatal trap for the naïve and unprepared.

The three princes departed once the sun hit a pole's length. They rode with the skill of the privileged nobles—blessed with both inherited talent and the best trainers who have been working with them since they were slightly older than infants. Nature and nurture. Clouds of dust from the pounding hooves rose to the air, blurring the sights of the audience, who cheered as loud as they could until they could no longer see the last glimpses of their heroes. Then they waited.

Right at noon, sounds of hoofbeats started to be audible from afar. Then clouds of dust wafted in the air, hailing the arrival of the three anticipated warriors. The mighty mounts galloped at top speed,

cutting past each other, each prince vying hard to keep his place at the
front. Finally, one mount sped past the rest. It was clearly Prince Ra,
galloping at a dash to enter the amphitheatre, crossing the finish line
with pride. Once affirmed the winner, Ra rode his mount around the
wide expanse of the arena, puffing out his chest with pride. The crowd
gave a deafening applause.

Sa followed as second, while you were last. Nobody bothered to pay
any special attention to either of you.

Prince Ra, the eldest son, the winning son, was lifted up high
and carried by soldiers to sit by the Ruler, next to his seat of honour.
You and Sa walked behind the procession, every step marred with the
pain of defeat. Sa glowered towards Ra, encapsulating him in his black
hateful gaze. The Ruler embraced his three sons, but of course the
longest grip was for Ra, as the winning son. Ra took his seat next to the
Ruler, while you and Sa sat behind him.

'This is a disaster,' Sa whispered into your ear, while sipping from
his golden cup.

You nodded in agreement and waited.

The Ruler's favourite beast, pet monster, was escorted into the
arena. *Cerberus*, all three heads intact. Its chain was loosened so the
monster could roam the amphitheatre. Its paws padded the dusty floor,
its three heads raised in alert. As soon as a deer was let loose in front
of it, the royal family and the audience were treated to a display of pure
savagery—swift, merciless, violent, how a true predator acted when
faced with its prey. The Ruler drank it all in, the spectacle before him,
clearly euphoric, his eyes glazed and his mouth slightly open. Perhaps
he was seeing his own reincarnation, walking the earth with three heads
and a mighty roar. Every movement was an art, every roar was a battle
cry, every slash of its claws was how a sword ought to swing.

When the deer fell, its hind legs twitching in pain and fear, waiting
for the jaws of *Cerberus* to shred its life to pieces, the crowd cheered
again. These people were addicted to splashes of blood and spectacles
of death, and their Ruler was not much different. He stood up, clapping
his hands and laughed aloud with so much satisfaction, one could
almost imagine he was the actual predator, holding a defenceless prey
in his jaws. Ra was absorbed in the spectacle, shouting in frenzy, while

Sa remained still, glowering. You noticed that only the right head of *Cerberus*, the eldest head named Ra, was devouring the succulent bloody flesh, while the other two heads watched.

'Feeding one head is enough to satisfy all three,' you whispered into Sa's left ear. He was silent for a while, his forehead wrinkled into a frown. You saw how both his hands trembled.

'Tonight,' the second prince whispered back. 'When the moon reached its peak, wait for me in the basement chamber. By the cage of *Cerberus*.'

You moved your head in a barely perceptible nod, and kept all your questions to yourself. What scheme were cooking up in your cunning brother's head? Throughout the rest of the day's festivals, not a smile crossed Sa's face. He did not make any effort to hide the desire for vengeance, so plainly scratched all over his face.

The next morning was catastrophic. The Sovereign Ruler trembled with barely contained anger. The wiry man whose body was full of scars, the caretaker of the *Cerberus*, crouched in fear in front of the Ruler. He reminded you of the poor deer about to be mauled by the *Cerberus*.

'How could Ra die?'

Up to that moment, all the terrified nobles in court were making wild guesses about the source of the Ruler's rage. They did suspect that it must have something to do with the *Cerberus*, but their imagination dared not touch the possibility of the death of one of its heads. Audible gasps spread through the court, and immediately stopped, leaving a gaping silence. Ra squirmed where he sat—the death of his namesake was definitely a bad omen for him. Your stolen glances towards Sa failed to detect any signs of guilt, nothing that could raise suspicions. His face was a mask of outrage and confusion, mimicking that of the Ruler.

'I do not know, o Ruler. This morning, when I opened its cage, the rightmost head was slumped at a strange angle, its tongue lolling out . . . the eyes open in a blank stare. It was dead,' the caretaker, normally poised and capable, was hardly able to string words together. 'There was a bruise encircling its neck, like a garrotte mark. It might have been strangulated to death.'

'I know what happened! I did not ask you to recount the damned story again. I want to know, who murdered Ra? Tell me!'

The caretaker spluttered some incomprehensible replies. This is a question he did not have the answer for, and his fear multiplied manifold. Ra, the Prince Ra, came to his rescue.

'Father, let me investigate this matter.'

This new situation was bad for his prospects; he must do something to remedy it.

The furious Ruler swallowed his words and walked silently out of the hall. He did not grace anyone with a look, not even Prince Ra's hopeful face. His breath was heavy and crackling, like the growl of a wounded animal. You noticed the faintest hint of a smile flickering on Sa's face.

'This is a royal secret. I don't want anyone outside this hall to find out. Not until the traitor is captured.' The Ruler gave his final order before disappearing from view.

The dead *Cerberus* head was decapitated, and was taken to be cremated deep in the forest. The caretaker treated the stump. Cleaning and stitching the wound of a wild beast was not an easy task.

The wild beast was no longer three-headed.

'Nothing but ill luck shall befall us all after this,' the caretaker said ominously, when you went to visit him by the underground cage. He was lucky to escape with his life after facing the Ruler's wrath.

Later that afternoon, the Ruler returned to good cheer, although sometimes you could see rage floating in to cloud his visage. The tournament between his three potential successors continued. You and your brothers were carried in palanquins, your arrivals cheered by enthusiastic supporters. Their shouts and screams show no decrease in euphoria, but you saw how uneasy Ra looked, and how unusually bright Sa was. You collected mental notes and folded them in little pieces to store at the back of your mind.

The second round of the tournament was an archery contest. The second prince, Sa, was going to shine the brightest. The accuracy of his aim was known throughout the empire. He never missed a target. His two brothers were also good archers, but neither could hit the bull's eye as sharply as Prince Sa.

The three princes took their positions at one end of the amphitheatre, standing strong facing the setting sun. Their eyes were blindfolded. Each were armed with a bow and three arrows. Ra held blue arrows, Sa was stroking his red arrows, while you were given yellow arrows. In the other end of the amphitheatre, several men stood guard over a huge wooden cage. Behind the ornamental carved bars, fifty birds of various sizes and species were chirping and hopping, flapping their wings futilely.

The only sounds audible in the amphitheatre were the birds chirping and the thousands of hearts beating in suspense.

Once the drumbeats begun, the guards opened the cage. All fifty birds stumbled over each other, rushing out to what they perceived as freedom, escaping into the open air in a noisy flurry of dust and feathers. You and your two brothers—the princes of the Empire—immediately took aim and shot the arrows towards the sky, first, second, and the last. This was not a mere test of raw skills—the princes were also being judged on the sharpness of their senses and the magic of their intuitions, requisite for a good ruler.

Moments passed and all the fortunate birds have escaped to the forests. The carcasses of the unfortunate ones lie lifeless on the ground, arrows of three colours stuck on their chests. The arrows and their victims were collected and brought before the Ruler to be counted in the open. Each of the dead birds were pulled from the shaft that took their lives.

'The blue arrow, belonging to Prince Ra, the eldest, killed six birds!' announced the first referee. Ra raised his hand to wave to the cheering crowd.

'The yellow arrow, belonging to Prince Ta, the youngest, also killed six birds!' the second referee announced. The crowd cheered louder. You bowed in respect.

'The red arrow, belonging to Prince Sa, the middle prince, killed eight birds!' the third referee boomed his announcement, which was received by a thunderous roar from the audience. The Ruler himself rose from his seat of honour and clapped. Sa raised both his hands, threw his head back and laughed with a roar like a winning prince should.

Prince Sa was escorted to the Ruler's side, who embraced him in a close grip. Prince Ra, the eldest prince who had just been defeated, couldn't hide his crimson face. The shame and resentment was a far cry from the pride that he savoured just yesterday, when he was crowned winner of the first contest.

It was now Sa's turn to have a seat by the Ruler's side. Drink from his royal father's cup. Share the meal from his dish. Prince Sa was clearly ecstatic with pride and pleasure, while his brother Ra watched from afar with gaze full of spite. That was when you took your cue. You approached Ra, and whispered. 'I knew who killed the first head of *Cerberus.*'

Ra was taken off guard. He stared at you with suspicion. You came close to his ear, and whispered, longer this time. His eyes bulged and reddened to match his bloodshot face, the capillaries in their whites pulsing with every word heard.

'Wait for me, tonight, by the cage of the *Cerberus,*' Ra whispered back, in a voice cracking with emotions barely held at bay.

You nodded, and remained silent and observant throughout the rest of the remaining celebration. The Ruler and Sa were drunk in festivities, while Ra was scheming.

The next morning was charred again by the wrath of the Ruler. The wiry caretaker was grabbed by one hand and lifted into the air. The Ruler was getting advanced in age, but his strength was still phenomenal, and his fury was never meant to be trifled with. The caretaker was convinced that his fate was as good as a deer trapped in the *Cerberus'* jaw—he was going to be a dead man soon.

'Who was trying to challenge me? After Ra, now Sa is dead!'

The Ruler bellowed.

No one dared to answer. Not even a whisper. To get in the way of the Ruler's rage was suicide. Prince Sa bit his lips, trying to contain his own anger, while glaring at you and Ra. But he could not voice out anything—he was the person who first poured poison, and it has now trickled into his own cup.

The Ruler, in his rage, began to hit and kick against the furniture and decorations in the royal assembly hall. He roared and swung his swords blindly, slashing against wood and iron. It barely missed the caretaker's carotid pulse—the hall was almost bathed in blood.

Nevertheless, the Ruler still retained some sense despite his blinding fury. If this small man lost his head, nobody else would be able to take care of the *Cerberus*. After demonstrating his rage, he left the hall without a word; a repeat of yesterday's episode. Of all the people left in the hall, the caretaker breathed the longest sigh of relief.

You realized that Sa was staring at you, while it was Ra's turn to suppress a smile.

'For twenty years *Cerberus* lived with three heads, but the heads never barked or bit at each other. Like the past, the present, and the future, each had its own path to follow, leading its own existence, independent of but in harmony with the others,' the caretaker spoke in mournful tones. He was cleaning faeces and blood splattering on the floor of the cage when you visited him that morning. The beast that used to have three heads was no longer special. Not three-headed, not even two-headed. It was merely a vicious, feral animal now, with one head like every other beast.

'Each understood its own roles and powers. They didn't fight over who should have what.'

You kept mum. You suspected that the caretaker knew more than he let out, perhaps he knew the secrets of the three princes. In silence, you watched the one-headed *Cerberus*, weakened after its multiple injuries, cradling its remaining head by its front legs, staring into the future that might be filled with chaos and regrets.

On the evening of the final tournament, the three princes were able to test themselves against each other in a three-way contest. A small, high wooden platform was built in the middle of the amphitheatre. You and your two brothers, who now harbour spite against each other, were readied with armours, shields, and the sharpest swords. Each could not wait to thrust their venomous blade into the other's chests. Let all long-harboured resentments gush out with life blood from the beating hearts.

You, Ta, the youngest prince, was always the best with your sword. Lightning reflexes, quick thrusts, and razor-sharp intuitions were your fighting style. Having as opponents your two emotionally disturbed brothers tilted the advantage further to your favour.

You began by letting Ra and Sa throwing aggression towards each other. The fight escalated quickly into a personal brawl. Every clang of blades was accompanied with spat out curses. Every deflected blow mocked with jeering words. The audience cheered even louder, driven into wild excitement to see such a spirited battle. You only butted in intermittently, almost lazily—the combat was almost exclusively between the two brothers. You let them exhaust themselves. It was too easy, you didn't even have to look hard to find openings. Ra slipped first from the high platform, falling to the ground below after missing his footing. Soon afterwards Sa was hurled down by your blow, crashing to eat dust.

The Ruler stood and joined the audience in a loud, long applause, apparently entertained by the display of his sons' combat skills. Now it was your turn to be carried and escorted like a victorious warrior. The Ruler embraced you so passionately, emanating a warmth you never experienced as his son before this. You were invited to sit next to him, and you truly enjoyed the position of honour. Even so, you did not allow yourself to lose your bearings. You were fully aware of the two pairs of envious eyes, shooting daggers behind your back.

'My royal sword, I present it to Prince Ta, in honour of his valour in battle. My blood flows in your veins, my son!'

You received the royal sword adorned with Black Gold and held it reverently. The hilt was gleaming with a golden sheen. Intricate patterns dotted with gemstones embellished its curves. You unsheathed the blade and swung it to and fro, slashing the air with poise, while the audience applauded. Behind you, Ra and Sa were whispering with each other—they seem to have forgotten their rivalry and united against a new common foe—you.

You folded another mental note to process, you have a new puzzle to solve. How can you win against these two, if they both conspire to bring you down? Meanwhile, the celebrations continued until the sun returned to its refuge between the mountains.

That night Ra and Sa sneaked into the underground chambers. The caretaker who was so determined to stand guard all night was given sedatives. He snored gently like a sleeping child, together with the three other guards. The royal sword bequeathed by the Ruler as his gift to you was hanging by Ra's waist.

'Silly Ta, he didn't seem to appreciate the value of this relic. He left if hanging by his door! I couldn't believe how easy it was to get it.' Ra chuckled, amazed at his perceived good fortune and your stupidity.

'Once this sword sticks by the *Cerberus*' neck, there would be nothing Ta could say to defend himself.'

In the steel cage, the one-headed *Cerberus* was half asleep. At the presence of Ra and Sa, it barely raised its remaining head. Perhaps the beast was drained of energy after losing two heads in two consecutive nights, perhaps the familiar scents and sounds coming from the two princes didn't raise its suspicions. Sa twisted a gear and a switch nearby, shortening the chain that kept the beast leashed. The chain tightened, *Cerberus* was rendered immobile. It barely noticed the change, the beast was not keen to make any movements.

'Thrust the blade to the base of its neck, cut the arteries. That will assure a quick and certain death,' Sa whispered.

Warily, Ra approached. The *Cerberus*'s head was big enough to fit his whole body in its jaw. He could smell the putrid breath, its wet warmth sticking on his skin. The red-yellow eyes glowered at him, the fire behind those eyes was fainter than usual but still burning.

Once he lifted the sword, ready to commit the deed, a blow landed on Ra's back. He collapsed immediately, losing consciousness. Outside the cage, Sa met the same fate before managing to put up any fight.

Cold water was poured on the princes, rudely dragging them up from oblivion. Ra opened his eyes weakly, then Sa followed suit. Both had their arms spread and bound to a pillory, their legs chained with irons. They glanced at each other, comprehension of their futile situation slowly dawning onto them.

'Traitor!' Ra and Sa trembled immediately, not from the cold water, but from recognition of the voice. The voice that commanded love, fear and respect since their infancy.

'The two of you were killing my favourite beast!'

'No, father. We were . . . ' Ra was at a loss of words.

'We were only trying to feed it, father. It was moaning with hunger,' Sa quickly picked up. It was a lame attempt, but at least he made an effort.

The Sovereign Ruler threw the stolen sword in front of their faces. The sword Ra took from your chamber. The two princes were dumbfounded. They couldn't say anything to save their pathetic lives.

You appeared and stood next to the Ruler.

'As I told you earlier today, I purposefully put the sword by the door of my chamber as bait. My guess was correct. These two princes were greedy and ungrateful. Treacherous sons, they were.'

'You...you traitor!' Your two brothers cried in astonishment. They immediately realized that they have been played, but like a lot of realizations, this one also came too late.

'The caretaker agreed to feed the beast tranquilizers and pretended to fall asleep. The traitors were these two princes, scheming to murder the Empire's beloved beast, the symbol of its power, the grace of its Ruler. I am the saviour,' you bent down and collected the sword adorned with Black Gold. With proper solemnity and ceremony, you presented the sword to the Ruler. This is your moment of victory!

'But Ta was also in on this, Father! He also took part in murdering the other two heads of *Cerberus*!'

You laughed in response. 'Haven't I told you that they were going to do this, Father? When trapped, rats will try to bite the cat. They will try to blame me, despite the glaring evidence to their crimes.'

Everything has been planned to perfection by you. The Ruler was drowning in his rage, there was no room in his heart for mercy or forgiveness. Prince Ra and Prince Sa wept and begged, but their deaths only inched closer with the passing seconds.

'There will be another contest tomorrow!' The Ruler meted out his sentence. 'Prince Ra and Prince Sa are going to fight the one-headed *Cerberus* —without shield, without armour. And without weapons!'

Ra and Sa were shaking so hard, their knees were barely holding them up.

In the silent palace hall, the *Cerberus'* roar could be heard—sending terror from deep down in the basement.

After Time 8: Hydra

YOU crept along, slowly.

It was a narrow crevice, pitch-dark and scattered with sharp stones, not an easy path for a sturdy man of robust build. The last time you passed this way was ten years ago, as a terrified child, shivering and alone. The secret passage brought you out of the burning hell that was devouring your closest and dearest. Through its darkness, you reached the bright light of survival. And tonight, you braved the passage again—but heading in the opposite direction.

You could feel the crawling insects and small animals who tried to get a taste of your flesh. You scratched and swished, and kept going. Sometimes a sharp sting made you wince, but you were not deterred, not even slowed down. There was no room for distractions. You must traverse the whole length of the passage—a hundred arms-length, give or take—before the night ends.

The entrance was hidden under the buttress root of a huge tree by the river. You must endure the narrow and spiralling tunnel to reach the deepest base of an underground cave, the lair of a serpentine reptile called the *Hydra*. The eight-headed serpent's slithering body was covered in iron-hard squamous scales and breathed poison. You were going to face it.

A few days ago, you approached the Ruler in his palace and volunteered to solve a ten-year-long problem which has plagued the nation with no apparent way out in sight. A phantom in the dark, the *Hydra* lied in its cave, waiting, sending echoing hisses that struck fear into the bravest of hearts. Anyone who dared to stand in front of the cave could hear the giant scales crashing against each other with crunching sounds like broken bones. They could hear loud wails like a kettle boiling. The more fortunate (or least?) ones could see shadows of the multiple heads, greenish-black, peering out of its hole, showing glimpses of the tongues and venomous fangs. Not to mention the chemical odour wafting and contaminating the air. A whiff or two, dum! People have been found unconscious, even dead, merely from the poisonous breaths.

Since the past ten years, the *Hydra* has inhabited the cave at the foot of the hill. It was not very far from the countryside palace of the Ruler, the place where he would reside when he was not hosting assemblies in the capital. On nights with full moon, the semi-aquatic monster would be seen swirling in the currents of the nearby river. Several times the locals stumbled into signs of its presence in the forests, probably looking for food. Livestock have been missing with nothing left but splashes of blood.

'For ten years my best warriors have tried to kill the monster. What made you think you could accomplish what they have failed to achieve?' the Ruler asked. He was a small man of stunted growth, but his voice boomed much larger than his minute size.

'I have been observing its behaviour and habitat for years. I know the *Hydra*.'

'Alright then. There is no harm in trying. But if you failed, I will personally throw you right in front of its eight heads!'

You knew the Ruler was making a show of his powers. You played along, and bowed with appropriate submissiveness.

'O Ruler, what if I made it? What will be your gracious reward?'

'Tell me anything you wish for. I will grant your wish.'

You were only a carpenter's assistant. Adopted and treated like a son, you helped him in his shop and learnt his craft. It was a humble but happy life. Your foster father was also a herbalist, for generations his family has been gathering the knowledge of poisons and remedies. As successor of the lineage, you took the learning in your stride as well. You became familiar with every flower, leaf, bean pod, and mushroom cap that littered the forest floor. In your repertoire of skills was also archery—you never missed your aim, you could read the comings and goings of the wind. You grew into a man of many talents. Your grim childhood was your best kept secret. Nobody needed to know about that.

Stories about the eight-headed giant serpent who guarded the cave has been repeated by citizens of the Empire so often, it was a living legend. The tales spread from mouth to mouth, city to city, then went to the villages and deeper rural settlements. Exaggerations and embellishments were added here and there, making the stories more mystifying, more thrilling. People made songs and metaphors of the *Hydra*. Most worrying to the Sovereign Ruler, the *Hydra* became a nemesis to the Empire, a challenge to defy him, and the grandeur of his opulent countryside palace.

Your foster father, the carpenter, told you his version of the story. According to him, settling in the valley below the hill now haunted by the monster was once a peaceful agrarian community. At that time, a little more than ten years ago, farms stretched green and prosperous in the valley. The people cultivated their lands and lived a quiet life—producing enough to feed themselves, with some extras to sell in the capital of the Empire. A river running across the valley blessed it with water and fertile sediments from its banks. No planted seed failed to sprout; every single tree produced fruits.

While occupied with their day-to-day motions, residents of the valley were surprised by the arrival of a crowd from the capital. An assemblage of sorts, they came on their horses and elephants, and included a hundred labourers. The Sovereign Ruler sent them here to set up tents, chop down trees, clear the forest and level the hillside.

'The Ruler desired a new palace here, by the foot of this hill,' a representative made the official statement.

The region greeted this news with joy. Who wouldn't feel honoured to be neighbours of the great Sovereign Ruler? Their lives must be going to get better, too—the benevolent Ruler would surely pay attention to their hardships and invite them to royal feasts. The villagers came to help in droves. They abandoned their routine in the farms to lend their hands in the clearing and construction work, to prove their undying loyalty to the Ruler.

'We must never offend the Ruler, we must not let him feel that we did not appreciate his presence,' so thought the earnest villagers.

Once the countryside palace stood in its glory, everyone could see that it was a testament to the Empire's wealth and the power of the Ruler. Every structure gleamed with luxury and magnificence. A grand archway stood centre to the fortress wall that stretched at the base of the hill. Landscape trees and decorated lanes were artfully arranged to penetrate and circulate the complex. Tunnels and air bridges crisscrossed like spider webs. Futuristic and avant-garde architecture. A landmark achievement for the Empire.

The villagers' excitement survived barely a few days after the official opening ceremony. They were never meant to partake in the splendour, not even from the outside. The Ruler passed orders that the villagers must be moved away, because their presence ruined the grandeur of the palatial complex. They were an eyesore, garbage that must be cleared. Furthermore, expansion plans were forthcoming. The team were going to construct elite residences and diplomatic centres in the surrounding area. The prestigious palace must be complemented with suitable fineries around it, and the villagers with their farmlands definitely did not fit the bill.

A terrible civil unrest rapidly ensued. The villagers rose in protest. They were given meagre compensations which could hardly support them in rebuilding their lives. They had to start over from scratch, because they were driven out of their homes with little more than the clothes on their backs. What begun as a peaceful demonstration transformed into an aggressive, physical showdown. There were many heartbreaks, and not a tiny amount of horror. People screamed, shouted and wept. Blood was shed. Chaos escalated, until one day everything was silent. No more noises or angry complaints from dissatisfied villagers. No more villagers, even. They disappeared in the blink of an eye.

You could now smell whiffs of the chemical-laden breath of the *Hydra*. Your head began to pound, and your eyes started to water. Your vision, already limited in the pitch-dark shaft, were dotted with stars. Those were signs that you were approaching the underbelly of the cave, where your quarry lied. Always well prepared, you took out a mask specially crafted to filter out the poisonous air. Alas, you could not cover your whole body. The toxin diffused onto the top layer of your skin, making you squirm with irritation and burning sensations. Hisses and faint wails grew louder. Your heart pounded faster.

Nobody knew this secret passageway. The diameter was too small. You found it by sheer luck, when you were trapped in the cave a long time ago. When you were desperately looking for a way out, and as soon as you found one, you crawled into it and squeezed yourself into what seemed like an endless tunnel, wiping tears and snot from your face and fervently praying to arrive somewhere you could breathe.

At the end of the tunnel, the adult you now cautiously peered into the lair of *Hydra*. The serpent laid in a massive coil on the cave floor, a monster emitting foul intent and fetid stench. The distance between you and the beast was too near, you could almost hear its own beating heart matching yours. It could not reach you when you were hidden in this tiny crevice—but it could still spray jets of venom from the valve underneath its tongues.

No time to waste. Making no sounds, you took out arrows forged from cast iron and copper. The sharp points would be able to penetrate almost anything—including the thick and calcified scales of the *Hydra*. Earlier, you had spent days to brew a poisonous potion, into which the tips were dipped. After that, you daubed a paralytic gelatinous mixture on their surfaces. The deadly combo of venom and weapon, that was your main bet.

A well-aimed shot went straight to the centre of the *Hydra*'s bulk. This was an ambush it did not anticipate. The *Hydra* began to thrash wildly. You shot the second arrow. The *Hydra* wailed, all eight heads releasing howls that could split eardrums, its massive serpentine form writhed and crashed against the cave walls in agony. The struggle persisted for a while, until its movements began to slow down and cease completely. Your poisonous arrows defeated the *Hydra*.

You grinned with glee, your mission was accomplished. Now it was time for you to retreat, shuffling backwards towards the hidden entrance from which you entered. The passage was too narrow for you to turn around. Leaving from the cave mouth, literally walking over the *Hydra*'s body was also too dangerous. Your luck could reverse, the poison may fail to complete its job, then the *Hydra* might open of its eight pairs of eyes, and that would be the end of you. Despite the awkward shuffle, your passage out of the tunnel felt significantly smoother and faster.

As soon as you were out of the pit, you hurried to the palace. Your presence was already awaited by twenty men with muscles, shields and spears.

'The *Hydra* is motionless in its lair! The *Hydra* is not moving anymore, waiting for you in its lair! Quick!' in your excitement, you shouted from afar, breathless with running. The moment those warriors heard your cries, they gathered their arsenal and rushed to the cave of the *Hydra*. They must verify your words, and the scene that greeted them in the cave confirmed that indeed, you, the humble carpenter's son, had triumphed over the monster.

There was no motion, no breath, no foul contaminated air.

As was the Empire custom, festivities were in order. The following night, the palatial complex was vibrant with celebrations. Commoners and nobles wandered the grounds freely, singing, dancing, engorging themselves on food and drinks, getting drunk. Colourful lights were lit from the top to the base of the hill, turning into a glittering mound if seen from a distance. Music played nonstop. Aristocrats, ambassadors and their family members were invited from all over the Empire and the neighbouring kingdoms. This must have been the biggest festival in this countryside palace, even grander than its opening ceremony ten years ago.

In the middle of the main hall, a six-feet high platform was constructed for the sole purpose of displaying the trophy—the *Hydra*'s ectothermic and frozen serpentine bulk, all eight heads slumped with no sign of life. 'As the pinnacle of tonight's celebration, we will decapitate all eight heads of the *Hydra*, and hung each head in every corner of the palace!' The Ruler announced, his pride restored, this most powerful monster now within his powers.

As for you, the Ruler seemed to not forget your role in capturing this monster. He showed you his gratitude through his multiple embraces, awarding you a handsome set of royal outfit, and inviting you to take a seat on his right hand side.

'Tonight is for you!' he shouted and patted you on the back. The Ruler was inebriated, like most of his subjects that night.

Well-fed and drunk, everyone was euphoric and generous with their congratulations. You lost count of the good wishes, praises and embraces that you received.

'Now, hero of the Empire,' the Ruler spoke out over the hubbub. Slowly, the noises dimmed down, those who danced concluded their moves, those who were drinking put their glasses down. All eyes gradually focused on you.

'What reward do you desire, after completing this impossible task?'

For a brief moment, you lost your composure. You did not expect this question to come in the middle of the party.

'Tell me your heartfelt wish, o hero of the Empire,' the Ruler repeated his question, a bit more forcefully.

You hesitated, and swallowed a few times. You pushed your seat backwards. Some extra space would be more comfortable.

'Before making my request, may I explain how I discovered the way to defeat the *Hydra*?' you spoke clearly, but only loud enough to be heard by the Ruler and his guests closest to the throne. Those further in the middle of the hall and near the door began to tiptoe and strain their ears to hear what was going on.

'Ten years ago, this hillside and its valley was a fertile land, where a community of peasants made their humble living. They were not wealthy, not by the Empire standards, but they were contented and happy.'

Your nervousness dissipating away, you spoke with more conviction. The Ruler frowned—something began to disturb the waters of his memory.

'Ten years ago, labourers from the city came to build a citadel of the Empire by this hill. Indeed, it was this very palace that we were standing in. The villagers were initially delighted. Their land was geographically desolate, forgotten at a corner of the Empire. Attention from the Ruler might bring forth a better life—they thought of a benevolent ruler watching over them, they thought this was the answer for their many prayers. But the lords in the palace shared none of their happy thoughts. They were regarded as nuisance. Their scattered huts were poor company for the grand palace, and must be replaced with mansions for aristocrats, rest houses for merchants, and holiday residences for the wealthy. The peasants were forced to relocate to places unknown, their meagre possessions seized, some were even kicked out of their abode in the midst of dinner, with food still in their hands.'

The Sovereign Ruler looked increasingly uneasy. One could believe that his seat was littered with small stones, the way he shifted and squirmed. The hall was completely silent, the guests trying their best to catch your every word.

'They resisted,' you sipped a glass of water, your confidence rising. 'The peasants fought hard to stay in the place where they were born and raised, and where they were raising their own children.' At that word, you faltered a bit, composed yourself, and continued.

'If they were driven away to seek their fortunes elsewhere, with no land to cultivate and build a home in, they would certainly perish. The dispossessed never survive very long. Realizing that their choices were only between fighting to stay or departing to die, they gave their all to defend their rights. However, a group of malnourished peasants armed with sticks, chipped axes and blunt machetes were no match to the palace guards complete with their inventory of weapons. Those who survived were rounded up, bound, and dragged to the cave by the hillside—the cave that we now knew as the *Hydra*'s lair.'

You paused, searching for the right words to continue your story.

'Then what happened?' a woman in the audience suddenly asked aloud.

'A bonfire was lit at the entrance of the cave, blocking the way out and filling the space with smoke. Thick, caustic smoke, bringing death slowly, heave by agonized heaves, their chests and throats lurching in vain trying to breathe. Their bodies were left to rot in the cave, the rank stench of decay attracting the *Hydra* who came from the deep. Once getting a taste of the surface creatures, the *Hydra* began to slither further into the outside world, terrorizing our lives.'

'Liar! If they all died, how did you know this story?' The Ruler exploded. He jumped to his feet, his hand reaching the sword hanging by his waist.

'When the palace was constructed, I was twelve years old. I was a scrawny, tiny child. In the cave, when the smoke was thickening, I managed to slip out of my bonds and crept further into the cave to look for a way out. I found a narrow crevice in the cave wall, my small body allowing me to squeeze into a tunnel which led to an opening under the roots of a tree not far from the river. Yes, I was once in the cave with my now dead family.'

Your final utterances snatched the Ruler's voice—he fell silent, his mouth opened and closed like a fish, but no word came out.

'I do not wish for anything from you, o Ruler. My only request was for the remains of the peasants, including my parents, which now lay scattered in the cave, be collected and laid to rest in an honourable place in the valley, where they used to live. Let them rest in a marked graveyard. That is all.'

'Liar!' the Ruler raged, and began to holler, throwing wild accusations. 'You were only trying to make me lose face, and disgrace the Empire! You must be a traitor, a spy from the enemy!'

You knew, in this open hall, in front of the thousands of guests, the Ruler could scream all he wanted, but he could not do anything too rash. At least for now, you were still relatively safe.

'That story was a lie, part of the myth surrounding the *Hydra*. Nothing but tales the uneducated folk told each other. The palace guards have gone to inspect the cave, and they found no human remains,' an advisor stood up and testified.

The lie did not upset you. You had expected nothing more honourable from these corrupted aristocrats.

'Now go away! If not because of your deed bringing in the *Hydra*'s carcass, I would have cast you to the deepest, darkest dungeon!'

Hastily, you grabbed your bow and herbal pouch, and made your way out of the palace. You did not want to press your luck; a good strategist always knew the best moment to put forth and to retreat. You were not going to stay much longer anyway. When the Ruler refused your request, point-blank, as you had expected, you knew what would transpire next. You had foreseen this long ago, it was a risk you decided to take—in honour of your beloved dead.

Most of the guests were confused of what was going on. They whispered among themselves, staring at you and stealing glances of the Ruler's flushed face. You walked straight out of the door, and only took one last look behind you—at the apparently lifeless figure of the *Hydra*.

'What I gave you was a curse, not a trophy,' you whispered.

Upon leaving the palace grounds, you hurried down the hill and crossed the river. It was an accursed palace, built with the bones of innocents, every brick permeated with the stench of their blood. You were keen to put as much distance as possible between you and the sepulchral building.

The sounds of music and merriment grew fainter and almost disappeared. Only your heartbeats were audible.

Tragedy was going to happen.

And it happened.

From where you were standing, safe on the other side of the river, you could see the palace erupting in a sudden flare. The wind carried to your ear screams and shouts, the sounds of pain and fear which must have matched those of the villagers left to suffocate ten years ago. You heard high pitched wails that still stung your eardrums even from afar. Scales crashing against each other like crunched bones.

'No poison could kill the *Hydra*, it was poison-made flesh. My arrows only rendered it paralyzed and unconscious for a while.'

You knew this was going to happen, you had planned it. Tears now flowing from your eyes were not for the decadent people and their Ruler being destroyed, but for the memory of your beloved dead.

'The *Hydra* is a curse. It was the vengeance of peasants against the merciless aristocrats. And now, father, mother, you are all avenged.'

After Time 9: Cyclops

'SIX years have passed with no conflict. Everyone has turned into weaklings, clinging to peace like it was their mother's skirts.'

The single eye at the centre of your brow flashed left and right, watching the other tribesmen, waiting for their responses. You squeezed your giant black hammer with your left hand, alternately loosening and tightening your grip. The hammer was your beating heart, you would never go anywhere without it.

'They trimmed their claws and shook each other' hands. King of the Western kingdom, and Ruler of the Empire in the East.' An older man spoke out in agreement.

'These people, they no longer have any need for weapons. What little remained in their arsenals were rendered blunt and rusty from years of neglect, only fit for volcano craters, or the underground dungeons, where the once-great swords and spears were buried forever.'

'But without wars, we will perish.'

'What else can we do?'

Hubbub ensued. From every corner of the room, several people had something to say, and the blend of voices rose higher to a clamour. Their useless banter enraged you. The rage surged through your bones and coursed through the veins of your arm, which you used to lift the hammer and crash it onto the rocky soil with a mighty blow. Literally shaken, the others went silent immediately. Every single pair of eyes was directed towards your fuming face, with a mixture of fear and anticipation.

'If there were no more wars, then we create one! Or two! Or more! It is us or them. Either we starve to death, or they battle to their deaths!'

Your tribesmen stared at each other. Their doubts were stronger than your conviction.

You were called *Cyclops,* but you were still part of the human race. *Homo sapiens.* Nothing about you was more or less than the rest of humanity—you had equally red blood, similarly beating heart. Nevertheless, you were not the same as them. You were different. Your single eye at the middle of the forehead, hulking stature twice bigger than ordinary humans, and deep guttural voice made you stand out like a deviation. Your people were regarded as monsters, half-blood humans, giants with the traits of beasts.

Nobody could accept your misshapen bodies, your bulging solitary eyes. Not the newly developed Kingdom in the West, or the citizens of the Eastern Empire. Hence, your ancestors sought sanctuary by this piece of forsaken land. They found safety in the most unlikely of places—mere miles next to an abandoned nuclear reactor, radiation still wafting from it in invisible fumes. The continuous fallout kept the *cyclopia* and *holoprosencephaly* mutation stay embedded in the genetics of these outcasts, and finally your people became a small tribe—all with one eye glaring from the middle of their forehead.

And the rest of humanity, those with two eyes, called you *Cyclops.*

While your minority tribe was struggling for survival, a huge war broke between the Western Kingdom and the Eastern Empire. Logic agrees that a ship cannot have two captains. Similarly, there could not be two thriving civilizations existing side by side without them clashing. At the top of the hierarchy, there was only space for one seat of power. The weaker party would be struck down by the stronger. Humans were stupid like that. *Homo idioticus.* True to those words, the *Cyclops* race have been lying on their faces for so long after being mercilessly clobbered by their non-brothers, their bloody desire for vengeance brewed more potent by time.

Nevertheless, war turned out to be an unexpected new rung in the survival ladder, inviting the *Cyclops* to climb. In their neglected corner of the world, they could hardly find food and other resources for life. The only substance they had in abundance was iron ore. There were hills above the ground composed of rocks so thickly intertwined with nodes of iron they looked red-purple. Underneath the surface your people found even more iron-infused rocks—magnetite, hematite, goethite, stretching far to the depths unimaginable. Armed with the iron-hard muscles they were born with, the *Cyclops* found their true calling. Like the Graeco-Roman mythical people who forged mythical weapons by the furnace of Hephaestus, they built swords, shields, axes, and chains with amazing artistry. Their huge fingers and calloused hands were as a dainty maiden's when it came to handling steel and blades. Gradually but surely, the forgotten people became renowned war engineers, pursued by envoys from both the West and the East, scrambling over each other to trade in weapons. For decades, stretching into centuries, the cycle continued. Their war fed your trade, and your trade fed their wars.

'But isn't it too cruel? We live on their blood.' A younger tribesman, whose nose was squashed flat at the centre of his face, muttered. He didn't raise his voice, it was barely a mumble, but your ears caught every single word.

'Our people did not know how to till the land or rear livestock. We were not hunters, neither were we familiar with the rivers and seas to fish. Trading with normal merchandise—food, silks, herbs, spices—is out of question, for we have none of them in the first place. We have been ironsmiths for so long, burning our hands and callousing our fingers, and there was nothing else we could do to survive.'

No one dared to answer you. Your calm tone could be deceptive; heads have been smashed, eyes have been blown by your outbursts.

'Listen. They, the people you were so sympathetic towards, never had the same feelings for us. They never bothered about our welfare, so why worry about theirs? Furthermore, they brought the disaster upon themselves. We never hurt them, but it was their ugly nature that led them to kill each other. The wars were their own doing. We *Cyclops* were the neutral observers, peddlers of weaponry, merchants selling the goods of war, merely fulfilling the requests of our customers.'

Convincing the rest of your tribesmen wasn't difficult. You had your arguments prepared early on, initially to silence your own doubts. Expressing them to soothe the conscience of others would be easy. Furthermore, the times were hard, and survival was always the priority.

Metallic clangs and thumps resounded in the air, while thick smoke steadily puffed out from rooftop vents, turning the air grey.

'The Western Kingdom was known with their double-headed arrows and wide-angled bows. The Eastern Empire would never go to battle without their curved long swords. We are going to need a hundred of each.'

Your orders were accepted without much questions. For five days and five nights, air surrounding the village and probably a few miles into the sky was grey and grimy with soot.

Every single able-bodied male joined in the effort. They divided into teams, each heading to a different area with specific tasks to do. One team moved to the quarry, mining the iron ores that have been lying untouched for six years. Another moved to the forest, looking for firewood to fuel the furnaces. There were teams dedicated to heat the ovens and arrange the equipment in their working order. Hopes were high. Your small community of forgotten people would have a chance to survive. In order to do that, everyone must chip in. For survival. 'All that we do is for survival,' you kept telling them.

'After this, what's next?' asked a young man, flat-nosed and sooty-faced like his brothers. He seemed a bit awkward with his tools. Perhaps the last time he learnt how to forge weapons was during his teenage years, when the bulk of his job would only involve chopping wood and smelting ore.

'The waters of the Western Kingdom have been terrorized by pirates for a while. They often attack and plunder the coastal villages. We would supply a hundred long swords with curved blades, the preferred weapon of the Eastern Empire.' You swung the glistening, freshly sculpted sword, to and fro, slicing the air. Amazing craftsmanship!

'The wide-angled bows and double-headed arrows, pride of the Western Kingdom, shall go to the rebellious and revolutionary factions in the Eastern Empire,' as you unveiled your schemes, you took aim with your single eye, and with a sharp whoosh the arrow glided through space to spike a distant wooden post. Right at the point you aimed.

It was not long before representatives from both sides fulfilled your invitation. They did not arrive without suspicions and questions, since dealing with the one-eyed giants was something they were not used to.

Rumours said that we *Cyclops* eat human flesh and drunk their blood to maintain our super strength. Anticipating a race of monsters, these pirates and rebels came fully armed, ready for violence and bloodshed.

When they returned to where they came, their arms were laden with gifts. The pirates from the West received a hundred swords, while the rebels from the east were given a hundred bows and arrows. They paid next to none for the transactions; your people told them that their goodwill was all that was needed as payment.

'So, what's next?' one of the flat-nosed, sooty-faced young men asked, not impertinently. You did not get angry. Rather smugly, you told him, and the rest of the people, to wait and see. To prepare all the materials necessary to keep the forges running.

Your predictions came true soon enough. Armed with their brand-new weapons, the pirates rampaged even wilder in the west, pillaging and murdering. Initially limited to their seaside territories, they cast their net wider, spreading violence in the villages deeper inland. They kidnapped young women, robbed farmers off their harvest, and burned houses. The Western Kingdom had to react in full force, sending thousands of their warriors in retaliation.

'Your Highness, we found these on the captured pirates. They look like the weapons of the Eastern Empire.'

Meanwhile, in the East, the rebels made optimum use of the double-headed arrows and wide angled bows. They became more efficient, better motivated. Strategic fortresses were seized easily. Empire garrisons fell to ambushes. Sentinels dropped dead without warning; double-headed arrows embedded in their necks.

'O Sovereign Ruler, these arrows belong to the Western Kingdom!' Seeds of mistrust and suspicion grew rapidly into full-blown war between the two civilizational giants—the Western Kingdom and the Eastern Empire. Confused citizens, unsure of the hows and whys of politics, were being drafted in droves. Healthy, able-bodied men were gathered in district posts and brought to the army barracks for recruitment. Fortresses were strengthened with fortified walls and arsenals. Warehouses were stocked with food, while ships were refurbished with new sails and supplies. Even the prison-houses were cleaned and emptied, ready to be filled with new captives. Both sides have been lulled with peace for too long. Like a long-chained beast forced into tameness, the animals inside these men were raring to sink their thirsty fangs into some bloody flesh.

Deep in the enclave of your people, you gladly received the messengers from the Western Kingdom and the Eastern Empire. You were well prepared for the guests—there were modest celebrations, good food, entertainment, and most importantly, deals for long-term contracts, ready for signatures and seals of royal approval.

In the privacy of your own room, you would occasionally succumb into fits of laughter. You couldn't believe how successful your plans had turned out to be. It wasn't a very sophisticated idea, rather, something hatched out rather urgently in a desperate situation. Now the two nations are really at war, with your people standing to obtain the most gains. Thousands of weaponries were ordered, which of course included the curved long swords and the double-headed arrows with their paired wide-angled bows.

Your people need not worry about poverty and hunger anymore. Food arrived in never-ending supplies. Silver, Black Gold, and luxury goods were delivered and piled up in increasingly higher heaps in the centre of the village. Nobody worried about thievery—everyone in the village had more than enough, and the rest of the world were too busy doing battles with each other. A proper place for storage could wait, you could build it later. The fates have turned. The *Cyclops*, once destitute, were now basking in prosperity.

Life in the village took on a new pulse. The tools began clanging a few moments before sunrise. The usual dry, cold air became warmer, heated by the furnace fires that flared continuously. Wood chopped and burnt, soil quarried from the mines. Everyone was busy at work, while savouring the fruits of those hard labour. The faces that used to be dull and lethargic were now brighter, while pounds of fat and muscles piled on the once emaciated frames. Indeed, the race of giants were transforming into real giants.

Meanwhile, battles and attacks were launched one after another in the distant coastal regions. Several times, the Western Kingdom managed to land their battleships ashore, reaching as far inland as they could to hit enemy forts, before being forced to retreat quickly.

Some other times, the Eastern Empire wrested control of the coastal region, establishing their hold behind their enemy's lines, before they too were forced to pull back.

Death manifested everywhere. Corpses in various states of decay and disfigurement laid forgotten, unmourned. Many of those bodies never received a proper funeral in the midst of battle. A lot of corpses were disposed of by weighing them with rocks and heaving them into the sea. Others were cremated, disintegrating into smoke, bone, and ash as blazing tongues of fire burnt the sky.

Deeper into the capital, poverty struck hard. Food had to be rationed. The economy was hopelessly crippled. One could hardly find a person who hadn't lost a family member. Most would have lost two or three. Children, women, confused old people, they easily slipped through the cracks, never to be found. Rage incited people to riots and rebellions. Death counts soared, even in places where no enemy forces invaded. The flames of war kept burning with no signs of subsiding, for months and months.

'When both of the great powers finally crumbled, our *Cyclops* race will lead a new civilization!'

You stood surrounded by mounds of treasures—Black Gold, silver, luxurious goods, all brought by the emissaries of both warring civilizations in exchange for the weapons they used to kill each other. You lifted your gaze to the sky, brimming with satisfaction, bursting with ambition. Definitely, you will not be the *Supreme Ruler* if you remained the humble ironsmith. Major changes were underway for you and your people. Great and fantastic changes. 'We will build grand palaces, luxurious houses. Smother ourselves in comforts. We have dwelled in squalor for many hundreds of years!'

Your people cheered. Every pumped-up sentence you shouted was received with hails and applauses. Why wouldn't they be jubilant? Why wouldn't they worship you? You saved your people from starving to death. You were their saviour. And this was what a saviour deserves: you began picturing yourself on a golden throne. Holding a staff carved from silver, studded with jewels and precious gemstones. The ceiling of your grand hall would be graced with chandeliers, the lightbulbs glittering like stars. The design should include a pool of crystal water with rainbow-coloured fish. You want a flag with your own crest, a *Cyclops'* singular eye, flying on tall masts standing in each corner.

And in your favourite version of this fantasy, you were standing on the rooftop of the tallest palace tower, gazing over the wide green expanse of land, all belonging to your people.

'Run! Save yourself!'

Your reverie was abruptly interrupted by the shouts and screams. The tribesmen gathering around were also bewildered. Before you figured out what was going on, a double-headed arrow swiftly found its way to pierce your chest, right through your heart.

'What does this mean?'

The twin arrowheads were designed to snag on the ribs and tear the lungs if the victim tries to pull it out. You let go of the shaft, and coughed out blood. Every breath burnt, and you could feel your heart heaving. Chaos descended upon your assembly. The *Cyclops* were running all over the place, trying to escape from the sudden attack. Smoke thickened, making your vision blurry. Houses and workshops went up in flames.

'So it was true. The *Cyclops* giants made a profit from war. You carved your wealth from our bones and flesh.'

Through your dying breaths, you could make out the features of the rebel leader who once received a hundred wide-angled bows with double-headed arrows from you. He crouched in front of you, his mouth curved into a mocking grin, his left hand firmly gripping a wide-angled bow.

'We like these long swords with curved blades. Your handiwork was excellent, no doubt. Too bad, you made the very weapon that will sever your neck.' A glistening blade sat menacingly next to your chin, its hilt in the hand of the pirate chief.

'We are very grateful for what you have provided. But all this wealth you've gathered are also useful for us. The Western Kingdom and Eastern Empire have proven to be too strong foes for small-time crooks like us.'

Your solitary eye blinked against the sun. You could hardly see anything against its fierce glare—perhaps fiercer than your ambition.

Zap!

After Time 10: The Slayer

THE sun glared into your eyes. For two weeks you have been hunkering in the dungeon, in one of the pitch-dark cells, where no light ever gets through, and so tiny an adult man has to bend his normally bent back even further in order to stand—and today, without warning, you were dragged out with chains weighing down your neck, hands, and feet. Even with your feeble steps, the chains clanged loudly, the only sounds tarnishing the otherwise silent morning.

It was a garden, damp from the dew and sweet with the scents of the morning blooms. A thin fog dispersed through the air. You felt swathed in a soft, cottony blanket of calm, temporarily erasing the pain you had gone through. Your rage, at least some of it, was put on hold. A small hut stood between the blooming bushes, where a man attired in black was sitting, apparently expecting you. He was sitting on a marble bench, which matched the marble slab propped up on ornately carved posts serving as a table in front of him. He stood up to receive you, and poured herbal tea into silver cups. The aroma was rich and earthy, with a sharp tang that reminded you of blood.

'Welcome o warrior. Please partake of these humble morsels I prepared for you. Simple they may be, but I assure you they are real delicacies. You must have been starving,' the words glided off his forked tongue, that you once swore to cut out after severing his neck. You swallowed your disgust, acknowledged your growling belly—you were still human, with human desires—and took the seat opposite his. You wanted to see where this would lead.

'For what do I merit this honour?'

'I just wanted to chat.' His charismatic mask was firmly in place, mouth curved into a smile. 'Of course, we shared a mutual animosity, and wished each other dead. You are the chief of rebels, in cahoots with the neighbouring kingdom, delusional enough to think you could revolutionize the Empire. Revolutionize me, it's Supreme Ruler. Such illusions deserve nothing but the death penalty, and that I have set in stone for you. But before the execution date, would it not be honourable for two sworn enemies to shake hands, clink our cups together and exchange words. Final words, for you, of course.'

You knew he was not giving a suggestion or offering a choice. You were a captured fighter, a wounded lion with amputated claws and bound legs. And you did not have much use for pride anymore.

'Please don't hurt my wife and my family.' The words came out as neither deferent or defiant, merely the voice of a defeated man. 'This is my final request. Please.'

He responded with a one-sided slant to his smile and a smug leer. A chessboard with black and white pieces has been sitting on the table next to the breakfast silverware, and he indicated them with his hands.

'Let's play chess.'

'I don't play chess. Chess is the game of aristocrats with too much time on their hands.'

'Don't give me your bluff. Any self-respecting strategist, war general, or rebel chief would not be a stranger to these pieces. Chess has been invaluable for political and military strategies since the ancient Persian and Indian times.'

You shrugged and raised your head, meeting his gaze. In front of the chessboard, you could pretend that he is your equal match, in a fair fight between warriors.

Your name brought nightmares to the Empire lords and aristocracy. At your peak notoriety, your name could bring shivers when spoken out loud, and bring hairs to stand on end when whispered. Like Midas creating gold with his touch, your hand could carry any weapon and change it into infallible killing instruments. Your opponents tend to turn into corpses after two moves. No enemy ever managed to stall you beyond two steps, with any weapon—be it a sword, knife, axe, spear, or a sledgehammer. You didn't know who started it, but soon you were known as the 'Two-steps Slayer'.

Your name went up rapidly to the top ranks of most wanted rebels. There was a bounty, rising steadily higher, placed on your head. At a young age, you have built a terrifying reputation among both the anti-ruler guerrillas and the Empire troopers charged with hunting you.

'Shall I start?' the Supreme Ruler moved his first pawn. Naturally, his were the white pieces. 'Tell me o warrior. Why did you despise me so much? Had you chosen the right side, you could have been a high-ranking general in the Empire army.'

'That was a rhetorical question.' You made your first move, too. 'You knew the answer. For generations, the Empire, with all its wealth and treasure, has been treated as the personal property of the rulers and their families. The time has come for the people to receive what is rightfully theirs.'

'You mean?'

'The people have their own rights on the wealth of the Empire. They deserve a share of the Empire's prosperity, a huge portion of which went to the plutocratic troves of the aristocracy.'

The long speech exhausted you. You haven't been speaking for a long time, and your throat was parched. You had to cut the diatribe shorter than you intended.

'The money came from the farmers, labourers, blacksmiths, and woodsmen.'

'The Empire needs money for governance, don't you think?' The Supreme Ruler kept the malicious leer pasted on his face. He must have thought he looked charming.

'What has the Empire achieved that justified such expenditures? Since the dam and amphitheatre were built several generations ago, there has been no real development for the people. The Empire has grown stagnant. No forward motion, no progress, in fact we were moving backwards with more corruption and crimes against the people.'

The Supreme Ruler chose not to answer immediately. He focused his gaze to the chess pieces. For a while, the two of you exchanged blows on the chessboard silently.

Like most other revolutionaries, the rebellion in you was also nurtured by the failures of the Empire. A poor boy who grew up watching his parents being tormented by the Empire bureaucrats, neck-deep in debts and astronomical taxes, struggling with ownership of their own patch of farmland that the officials were so keen to put their paws on. Poverty escalated into destitution. The rotten socio-political mechanism did its work as expected, as a totalitarian machine that has been recycled from the past, to reappear pervasively in these post-historic times.

The people were kept ignorant and uneducated to halt social mobility, to keep everyone on their own level of the social hierarchy. After the construction of the dam and the giant amphitheatre so many years ago, the previous ruler had burnt all books and declared reading an illegal activity. The great technologies from the past were not handed down to the next generations. The people were only told what they needed to know, taught what they needed to learn, just enough to create obedient servants to the Empire aristocracy. They were *Homo neophobus*. Too much knowledge is treachery, that was the unofficial Empire motto.

The totalitarian claw clenched even harder when the Empire began to micromanage the positions and roles of individuals in the society. Every person assigned to jobs where they would be most needed, according the Empire officials' assessments. Every marriage needs government approval. Farm boy to farm girl, daughter of an ironmonger to the son of another ironmonger. Families of tradesmen are only allowed to marry into other tradesmen's families. Aristocrats for aristocrats, definitely. The people shouldn't have too much variety, shouldn't be confused with too much choices. Confused people spoiled by too much choices would only serve to weaken the Empire.

Within the scheme, your role was predetermined to be a woodsman in the northern deltas of the Empire. Your brothers were scattered all over the land, assigned various menial jobs to keep the farms and industries going.

You chose to abandon the woods and raise your axe as a fighter. Together with other dissatisfied men and women, you decided that only freedom would make life worth living. Later, you learnt swordsmanship and mastered the use of other weapons. You were a natural with sharp blades and pointed tools, and you gained your nickname as the

'Two-step Slayer' within a few years' time. Your charisma grew too, from a quiet farm boy to a fiery leader. In your booming, hair-raising voice, you told your comrades that there will be no more silence. No more acting as brainless tools of the Empire. No more slavery and oppression. We are the *Homo independens*.

'Chess taught us many lessons.' He was intent on planning his moves, each piece carefully lifted after long deliberations.

'I don't learn from games. My great master who taught me about life is life itself.'

He laughed at your dismissal.

'A politician like me sees the chessboard as a mirror representing life. A Ruler, a competent one—not necessarily benevolent, ah hah—should have the bird's eye view of his empire, seeing each separate conflict as part of a big picture. A chess player does not only see his own pawns, but analyses the enemy formation. He must not miss even one small potential threat, one possible opening. Therefore, I know you much better than you thought I do, o warrior.'

You leaned back in surprise, slightly distancing yourself from the chessboard.

'For five years I have investigated about you. I could say that I learnt more about you, than I did about the backyard of my own palace. I know every scar on your body, where do they come from. Every history, every nostalgia that shaped this man you are now. Your father, lost in the currents when the village was flooded. Your mother, breaking her back in a farm at the south to raise three children. And the three children—you, sent to the woods in the north, your brother who became an ironmonger in the east, and your sister, who was arranged to marry a pastry maker in the west, so she could work in the fruit farms there. Great idea, isn't it? It worked for almost every family—tear them apart so the people have less bonds to keep them together, no bonds other than that of servitude to the Empire.'

Your heart began to beat faster. Fear was not an emotion you were familiar with. You used to be unfazed by the prospect of death or torture. Nevertheless, the Ruler's revelations—and the possibility of even more reveals, for obviously he was going to tell you more—struck shards of terror into your heart.

'You're mad!'

The Ruler ignored your outburst, and continued to play, muttering in a voice loud enough for you to hear.

'The strength of a chess player does not lie on what he currently holds in his hands, but on seeing the future. He has to predict what lies several steps ahead. You, the Two-step Slayer, finished off your opponents in two quick moves. You acted without planning. For you, things happened too fast, there was neither a room nor a need for plans. Terrifying indeed, but not practical for a long-term struggle. That was why, now I am sitting with you here, still in power, offering you a drink, while you are just a caged animal.'

'Did you really think so, Supreme Ruler?' Your turn to smile. Your enemy underestimated you too much, it seems. Underestimation usually demands a high price. Three moves of your knight across the board, and the Ruler lost two of his pieces. One bishop, and one pawn. You returned his smirk, but the Ruler showed no reaction.

'You still don't get it, warrior. Controlling the future does not mean achieving early victories, but making small sacrifices now for greater gains later.' Your eyes and his met again, both of you gazing more intensely into each other's eyes. He lifted his right brow, and felt disgusted at his shameless display of cunning. 'Remember when you were attacking a small Empire fortress in a northern hillside, more than a year ago? Wasn't it strange, a little bit suspicious, that the attack was so easily executed, with so much gains on your side? Were the Empire defences really that fragile? Did you not suspect anything at all?' The questions bombarded you, like little bullets. 'You may guess where actually the tip-off you received came from. Ah, the fifty Empire soldiers we lost were nothing compared to your head that we now possess.'

You were silent, trying to process the bullets one by one. Your memory unfolded slowly.

That was the first attack you ever led. You were with twenty other rebels, all of you young, hot-blooded, mostly inexperienced. Most of your comrades had never witnessed death in a battlefield. Their weapons were still virginal, unsullied by blood. Never seared any skin or torn any flesh. The strengths of the small gang include their fiery spirits, youthful energy, and a notorious murderer called 'Two-step Slayer'.

You received information through the vines, that several dozens of strongboxes containing tax collections from several districts will be stored in the fortress. The complex was quite simply constructed, with several partitions for storage and barracks for the guards. Coincidentally, a day earlier, the Empire soldiers were marshalled to the borderlands in response to impending Western Kingdom invasion. They brought with them all their best weapons and warriors, which exposed certain less important spots, like the fortress, vulnerable to attack.

The raid happened fast. Right at midnight, all torches were extinguished on cue. Even the moon cooperated with your plan, she hid behind the clouds, rendering the darkness total. The clang of swords and the slash of blades against flesh were interspersed with human screams. Blood drenched the night. The enemy was fighting blind, but your eyes were accustomed to the dark. One enemy head for every two steps. You knew the Empire soldiers were panicking, and you could smell triumph underneath the mingled odours of sweat, blood, and fear.

You stumbled against her in the chaos. Her fragile neck was almost ripped by your bloody sword, had you continued with your second step. In the faint light of the moonlight, partially appearing from behind the clouds, you could make out her features. She has blue eyes. Her face was smeared with dirt, her clothes shabby and bloodstained from where she had been wounded.

'I'm just a maid, a cleaner in this place. Please don't kill me.' She managed to utter with a trembling voice, before falling unconscious. You took her in your arms, for the first time you were that close to a woman. Close enough to notice her small eyes, now closed, and the fair skin underneath the grime. Your sword slipped out of your grip. The first person who managed to terminate your two steps of death was a woman without a weapon.

The booty from the raid was gathered in one place, and divided according to plan. A portion was given to the poor people of the North. Another portion was dedicated for the revolution. The fortress was dismantled, and together with the enemy corpses, was burnt to ashes.

With your two strong arms, you carried the girl back to the forest, to the secret hideout of the rebels. You knew, this encounter would change your life.

Women had never been more than a nuisance for you, a distraction, sometimes nice to look at, but ultimately not significant. Like rocks in the middle of a stream. You never talked about women, neither have you ever fantasized about having one. You knew sometimes women looked at you with desire, but you regarded them like overly affectionate cats—you didn't kick them away, but you wouldn't take them home with you either. You were a warrior, through and through. You talked about blood, battles, and death. You romanced swords and trusted spears.

That night, your sword slipped out of your grip.

You took care of her for three days. Her name was Su. She lost too much blood, her fair skin was rendered ashen, and her limbs barely able to move. She was a victim, trapped in the battle between the rebels and the Empire. Between you and the Ruler. Guilt seeped into the cracks of your heart.

She was born into servitude in the palace, like her parents were. Her purpose of life was to cook and clean. When she grew older, they sent her to the fortress with other girls of her age—to cook and clean for the soldiers there, and perhaps provide other services, as requested by the lonely men. She never questioned her roles—that was what her parents did, and her grandparents too. Their place in the social hierarchy was predetermined and not to be challenged. She was not a fighter like you.

'Su, you could go if you want. Your wounds are completely healed now.'

She has been staying in the hideout for three weeks. Your comrades have started to whisper, even to complain out loud, that you were getting closer to her, and further from the goals of the revolution.

'Do you really want me to do that? To leave?'

'What I want does not matter. I don't want much out of life, anyway.'

'So, if not for your own personal wants, why do you fight? Why do you put your life on the line?'

'For freedom. For the sake of freedom, I live and I die.'

'But don't you see, this fight for freedom has made a captive of you. You are not a prisoner with no rights, no future, no desires. True freedom is when you are brave enough to admit, that you do want something for yourself.'

'What should I want?'

'Anything. Love, maybe.'

Her smile cut right through your walls, leaving you exposed, undefended. You knew how it felt like to unsheathe your sword and slash into human flesh. Now you knew how it felt to be on the other end of the sword, when your own heart was sliced open.

Love turned your impenetrable fortress into a thatched hut in a storm.

'What a romantic encounter! How amazing! The warrior and his woman!'

The Supreme Ruler laughed obscenely. His whole body shook, his face distorted into grotesque grimaces, as if your private life was the funniest joke he has ever found. Your terror transmuted into rage, which rapidly reverted into fear, when you realized your helplessness. Of course, two weeks in the dungeons haven't done much to ruin your physique. You were still the 'Two-step Slayer'. The stupid chains wouldn't actually prevent you from snapping his neck with your bare hands.

But you were restrained by more than mere chains.

'Please. O Supreme Ruler, do not harm Su and our son,' you tried to keep your voice low and submissive. A wounded lion with amputated claws and bound legs has no use of a roar.

The Ruler pretended not to hear your pleas. He smirked and returned his attention to the chessboard.

'In the game of chess, the King was allowed the most limited range of movement. Meanwhile, each minister, bishop, and knight has somewhat stronger power. They were able to go anywhere they wanted on the board.' He took one of his white knights, and ran his index finger along the finely carved curves. 'What a clever trick. One might think that the courtiers hold all the power, but actually, the King holds supremacy above them all. Every single one of the courtiers are tools, disposable ones, with the sole aim to protect the King. This is a fact that many players have ignored and as a result, they were deceived even before the game begins.'

'Wouldn't you call that sacrifice, cooperation and loyalty?' You disagreed. You found it difficult to accept that someone, even as despicable as the Ruler, could be a total self-serving opportunist with no regard for other human beings.

'Loyalty was also just a tool for a Ruler. You name it. Patriotism. Unity. Peace. Justice. Every single one of those concepts, was meant as part of an eclectic propaganda. They made serving the Empire more meaningful for the servants, although in reality, the Supreme Ruler has absolutely no use whatsoever for the people.'

You ceased your attempts to see him as a fellow human being. He definitely met all the negative stereotypes that his enemies believed about him. Behind the smiling façade, he really was a monster with a filthy soul and black ambitions.

'Look at how I baited you, o warrior. A board of chess, translated into real life. Me, the King, sacrificing his ministers and advisors to trick you into lowering your defences. So we could come and get you.'

You could not deny his cunning. You were not yet sure of how he did it, but your presence in front of him, in chains, was proof that his plans worked.

A few weeks ago, news began to spread through the vines about the Ruler and the best Empire warriors going to reconnoitre a south-eastern city after its alleged raid by the rebels. The way there will involve going through a narrow mountain pass, enclosed on either side by cliffs jagged with rocks. Nature was going to cooperate in your endeavour to destroy the Ruler.

'The Ruler has no male heir. He only has a young daughter. Once we killed him, the dynasty would be left without a successor, and the government in disarray. That would be the best circumstance for us to establish a democracy, a people's republic.'

The rebel chiefs did not take long to agree on a plan. The opportunity was too good, extremely rare, unlikely to happen again very soon. The Supreme Ruler, despite his courageous veneer, was a coward. He almost never travelled out of his fortified capital, let alone going on a perilous journey to a rebel-infested region. Most of the time, he would despatch his servants and sycophants to do any royal or military errands. You weren't sure why did he change his mind that time, and neither were your fellow rebels. Most of you theorized that the Ruler wanted to reaffirm his image among the people, show his worthiness as a leader, and wrest back support that the people have been increasingly giving to the rebels. Explanations and theories aside, the revolutionaries were beyond keen to pounce on this occasion. Every single guerrilla will be gathered and placed into position. This attack must succeed, by any means.

Su, by then a mother, cradled your one-week-old infant in her arms. Her face was clouded with worry.

'Dear, please . . . enough of your men were going, they will win the battle. You can stay here with me, with our son.'

'But I've been waiting for this chance, for . . . for my whole life.'

'I need you by my side. Our son needs you. We need you more, than the other men in the battlefield needed you.'

For the umpteenth time, her pleading eyes shattered your resolve. When you shifted your gaze to the bundle she was rocking gently, what was left of it crumbled into dust. His resemblance to you was striking, and it was, as if, really you in her arms, who were given a second chance to be loved and nurtured in her embrace.

The rebel hideout in the woods was almost deserted, with only the injured and the invalids left. You were there, with the women and children who continued their domestic routines as usual. You felt guilty not to join your comrades, and you knew they called you a coward. They spat behind your back, saying that a woman and a child has rendered you an impotent warrior. You knew you let them down, but you couldn't leave your beloved wife alone. Not when she has just given birth to your son, and could barely stand on her own.

A few hours after the cooking fires have died down to embers, you were rudely snapped out of slumber by shouts and screams. It begun as distant, isolated shrieks, which gradually became closer and louder, spreading like wildfire. You could hear women wailing and children crying.

'We're under attack!' You whispered. Su, already awake next to you, trembled in fear.

First, you hid Su and your son in a small dugout hidden beneath a trapdoor on the earthen floor of your room. Once they were safe inside, you replaced the well-worn mat that used to sit over the place, and dragged the bed above it for good measure.

Second, you snatched your two swords. You put on your boots. You grabbed your two knives and holstered them on your waistband.

Third, you extinguished the remaining torches and stepped on the burning coals, letting darkness swathe the area. Without lights apart from the stars, advantage would be on your side. One by one, Empire soldiers fell as headless corpses and disembowelled cadavers. Not more than two steps for each intruder. You moved like a shadow, taking lives and delivering deaths like an angel with no mercy.

Nevertheless, the Empire came prepared. They sent 200 soldiers for a village that has almost no men to guard it.

You were a lion, but even a lion could be cornered into a trap.

'I lost two of my favourite advisors in that godforsaken south-eastern city. The rebels were very keen to see me dead. Talk about a good investment!' The Ruler broke into a loud guffaw as he watched you knock, in three successive moves, two more of his chess pieces.

'You purposefully sent them there? As bait?'

'Of course. They were only pawns in the game. They have been fattening their bellies for so long in the palace, the least they could do to be useful was become sitting ducks for you rebels.'

'You're heartless.'

'No, I'm a visionary. Come o warrior, pay attention to the board. Our game of chess was approaching its end.'

He sipped his remaining herbal tea, still warm in its silver cup. His expression remained smug, there was no trace of guilt upon recalling the fates of his two sacrificed advisors.

'Here's the final lesson for you.' He picked up one of his chess pieces, and proffered it to you. You watched impassively, and he replaced the piece back on the board. 'You see, the Queen seemed to be the most powerful character. She could move anywhere she pleased. In a flash, she could change the direction of a game. This game is not meant for mere idleness, o warrior. It reflects the reality of life, and it teaches important lessons about life. An otherwise undefeatable killer, would find his eventual demise by the delicate hands of a woman.'

You had a bad feeling about this, but you refused to analyse the Ruler's chatter anymore. You wanted to get the game over and done with quickly. You foresaw victory in several more steps—at least, on this chessboard, you could crush the Ruler's pride.

'Careful o warrior, when you feel that victory was close. Even the Queen was just a chess piece, subject to the whims of whoever was controlling the game. She could be manipulated. Like any woman. Like your precious Su.'

Out of nowhere, your Queen was taken over by the Ruler's bishop. Your King was placed in a checkmate.

You lost.

The victory you sensed dissolved into thin air. The Supreme Ruler heaved a sigh of satisfaction. You didn't feel any palpable sense of loss—you had lost enough, you couldn't possibly lose more. There was only one thing you wished for, and for the third time, you humbled yourself to ask for it.

'O Supreme Ruler, congratulations for your victory. You've had the game you wanted. You've said what you wanted to tell. You already have my life in your hands. Do with me as you wish, but please let my wife and son go. Don't harm them.'

'You're thicker than I thought. You rebels are all brawn, and no brain, aren't you?'

The bad feeling inside your gut worsened. Whatever was coming, you would not like it.

With a sinister grin, the Ruler signalled to one of the guards surrounding the hut. The guard disappeared behind the bushes, heading towards the front hall of the palace which directly opened to the garden.

A few moments later, a woman walked slowly from that direction, carrying a silver platter laden with fruits. She was small and graceful, with a familiar gait. She walked like a willow swaying in the wind. As she approached, you could smell her flowery scent. A white shawl, made of silk and trimmed with lace, covered her head and part of her face.

She collected the chess pieces, pushed the board aside, and served the platter of fruits on its place. Then your eyes met hers.

Her small, blue eyes. Now red-rimmed and brimming with tears.

'Su?'

'Su, my only daughter. Thank you for your gift of a male heir.' The Ruler gazed upon your horror-stricken face. 'Look at you. Try to look a bit proud! Ah, what an ideal successor for my dynasty. He would inherit his mother's beauty and his father's strength. And of course, his grandfather's cunning!'

Your sword has slipped from your grip, and sliced your heart to pieces. Love turned your impenetrable fortress into a thatched hut in a storm, and the storm has blown everything away.

You wept like a child. You couldn't believe that it was all a game. The love that you gave your life for, was just a series of premeditated moves on a chessboard.

The woman suppressed a sob, her shoulders quivering. Then she walked away without looking back, slowly disappearing into the lingering mist, the last of her scent mocking you with each breath.

You were a wounded lion that has finally surrendered to its chains, with no more will or reason to live.

After Time 11: Saliva

'TELL us from the beginning. We want to understand.'

You fidgeted restlessly, scratched your hips and back. Several moments ago, you had leapt into the yard, agitated and hysterical. 'The Ruler and his people were coming here. They want to give us offers.' The others who had been lounging on a nearby porch, shaded from the afternoon heat, were all sprung into attention.

'Tell us the story from the beginning. We want to know what was going on.' One of them insisted.

Everyone actually knew how the story had begun. You were part of a history, that was not history. A piece of time taken out of time. None of you who existed there, was recognized as existing. In the ghetto, that was a fact that everyone understood. No one outside the place wanted to remember your existence, that your people were once born as fellow human beings. The world consisted of earth and sky, sun and moon, man and beast, but never you. You were the edges of a shadow, appearing and vanishing without being noticed. Forsaken, disowned, and dispossessed.

The folks of the ghetto were worse than pariahs.

Thirty years ago, you were a normal kid with a happy childhood. Your family lived modestly, growing bananas by the foothills of the north-eastern mountain range. The best memories you had were of playing between the banana trees, going up and down the lower mountain slopes, without a worry in the world apart from your parents' screaming if you came home too late after sundown.

A terrible hurricane destroyed everything. Your humble house, the family farm and every plot of cultivated land around it, everything you hold dear, all shredded to pieces by the merciless storm. After the catastrophe, the ground that used to be so fertile, became cursed with soggy barrenness. Nothing fruitful ever grew, while the soil turned into slimy dark mulch, thick with filth from carrion, corpses and excrements. Those who managed to survive had to make do with barely human standards of living—hardly any food, makeshift shelters, and of course, the omnipresent filth.

Nobody came to help. Nobody from the neighbouring districts, nobody from the government, nobody from the Empire capital.

Days turned into weeks, and a new problem emerged. People began to find lesions on their bodies—brownish sores that rapidly turned black and festering with pus. Maggots appeared in the wounds, which spread to the whole body including the lips, nose and eyes. Bellies swelled with toxic gas, gums bled and teeth fell out. Many of those who somehow survived the initial assault, failed to withstand the sickness. Dead bodies began to pile up again, and word got out about a new plague spreading from the area.

Empire citizens from neighbouring cities started to panic. Natural disasters were common, some people were just unfortunate; but plagues were different. Plagues can spread, and looking at the way it ravaged the community at the mountain foothills, it wouldn't be long before the neighbouring cities and finally the whole Empire became infected as well.

'We must not let the plague pass beyond the area.' The Supreme Ruler passed his decree. A thousand soldiers were assembled for a siege. Wooden fences fortified with barbed wire were constructed. Emergency was declared, and no one was allowed to escape on pain of death.

Hunger and sickness made people desperate, while desperation brought madness. Not the barbed wires nor threat of death served as powerful enough deterrent. The quarantined people still attempted to escape. They looked for less guarded spots, then with basic farming and kitchen tools, they cut the barbed wires and tried to break the wooden fences. Hastily constructed, the barriers weren't very tough, and quite easily overcame by a few determined people, the agile ones wrapping their hands and feet with cloth before climbing out.

However, their escapade was short-lived. Empire soldiers stood at the ready—with arrows, swords, spears, and torches. Their choice was to retreat or to die, and most chose the latter. Better die a quick, bloody death, than to perish slowly inside the hellish enclosure. Soon, more desperate villagers attempted to crash the barriers, with little regard to whether they would live or die. All they wanted was to get out, and they did so in droves, overwhelming the soldiers who stood guard. The Ruler, not wanting to waste more of his precious military assets for some unimportant villagers, passed his final order.

'Kill them all. Kill everybody in the plague-infested area.'

It was a genocide. *Homo necans!* The whole region was incinerated. The destruction was absolute. It was, as if, man was telling nature that the hurricane one month ago wasn't cruel enough, and they themselves were going to finish the job. The night was ablaze with fire, fuelled by flesh and bones, of the already dead and the burnt alive.

You and a handful of others, the luckier, more resourceful ones, managed to flee from the inferno. Upon realizing that the Empire soldiers were going to destroy the area, you went to hide in the worst, wettest patch of land, farthest from the village front. That was where dead bodies and rotten waste were dumped by those who still had the will to impose some semblance of order into their lives, instead of just continuing to live in the filth.

As the Empire soldiers were rounding up the villagers and starting fires, your small group retreated further into the mountain woods, away from civilized lands, braving the dark night. The fifty or so escapees—men, women, children—stumbled on blindly, as far as their legs could carry them, until the sun rose and crossed the sky, and no one could walk a step further. The woods were thick with bushes and shrubbery, most of which were unfamiliar. The strange animals were intriguing and frightening.

Your people were raised to plant bananas in farms, not forage in the forest. Nevertheless, there was not much options left—there was no civilization waiting for you out there. You had to build your own life, separate from those who had cast you away. Gradually, the patch of land grew into a ghetto, a place where your people lead an isolated existence. Life in the Empire moved along without you.

'Let them be. As long as they stayed there, and didn't bring their filth anywhere else. Sooner or later, Nature will do away with them.' So said the Supreme Ruler. Indeed, living closely embraced by the arms of Nature was painful. Death, hunger, danger, and illness slipped in and out of your dreams, as if encountering them in your daily waking life was not enough. Food was scarce. The most abundant edible in that part of the forest was a purplish-blue wild berry, which you grabbed with both hands and ate with relish.

Death didn't seem to come for you, despite the destitution you lived in. You stayed alive. Your people stayed alive. Even better, the wounds and weeping sores on your limbs, trunks, faces, and scalps started to dry up, scab over, and eventually the scabs fell away to reveal smooth, healthy skin. Nevertheless, your status as outcasts remained so.

'For thirty years they pretended we didn't exist. We were never included in the social hierarchy of the Empire,' you sighed.

'They only think of us whenever they wanted to perform their stupid superstition. I don't know which deity would grant them their wish, but apparently many people out there believed that spitting ten times at us would remove their bad luck. Not even animals were subjected to this kind of humiliation.' A friend chipped in, words slightly muffled by the mouthful of blueberries he was chewing.

For the past thirty years, the ghetto survived in isolation, never recognized by the Empire. The names of your people and your place were taboos, forbidden to be mentioned. The soil was impure. The air was impure. Anything that grew on the land was impure. It goes without saying that the inhabitants of the ghetto, you and your people, were impure. Untouchables. If, by any accident, a normal, upstanding citizen of the Empire came into contact with the untouchables, he or she should soak for a whole day in seawater or saltwater to remove the contamination. Any animal or livestock that wandered into the ghetto must be killed and burned, no longer fit for human consumption.

Such were the curse that befell you!

'Hey, you haven't told us the story yet. We want to understand.' Your people began to lose their patience.

You scratched your body, trying to get between the thick, stringy hair. The more excited you felt, the more itches you needed to scratch first. The people of the ghetto may be as clever and articulate as ordinary citizens out there, but life in the forest never had much use for appearances—hence most of you were strangers to grooming and hygiene. The odour wafting from your unwashed body and lice crawling between the unkempt hair was typical for a common ghetto-dweller.

'Well, let's start with what we know. We are all aware, aren't we, that the Empire is being swept by a disease epidemic?' You began, as your friends listened attentively. 'This disease was horrible. Sores appeared on the body—all parts of it—brown-black sores, which quickly festered with pus and maggots. The stench was worse than rotten flesh. Parasites laid eggs in the livers and brains of the sufferers, and once that happened, they were as good as dead.'

'Is that true? The last I heard of such a disease would be . . . thirty years ago, when we were driven out here . . . ' one of the older folks commented.

'Yeah. Yeah. The difference this time, instead of just attacking a small group of people like us, the disease spread all over the city, too fast to control. Almost nobody escaped it, not even the palace people, not even the Ruler himself. No one managed to find a cure. The greatest palace doctors, all of them admitted defeat.'

'So why would the Ruler want to come to this place? What does it have to do with the epidemic?' someone butted in impatiently, and you told him off.

'Be quiet! Let me finish my story, would you?'

Five days ago, several afflicted people from the city went to the ghetto. They hung around the edges, spitting multiple times in the hopes of removing the bad luck. One of them spat right onto your face. Shocked and furious, you spat back onto his face.

'Are you crazy? If the Ruler knew about this, they will kill us and burn us!'

You, the ghetto-dwellers were just supposed to grin and let the clean, normal city people do what they wished unto you. If they wanted to spit on your face, you should happily allow them to do that. Being permitted to live was already too great a privilege, apparently.

Yet at that time, you were angered out of your senses. The man you spat on punched you, and his friends also took part in the scuffle that ensued. You ultimately lost, as you were alone, and nobody from the ghetto was willing to help. Your hands and feet bound with chains, you were dragged to the city prison. They said that they could have killed you then and there, but letting you starve to death among the rotting corpses and animal carcasses in the cells would be a more suitable punishment.

In the prison cell you were never sure of the passage of time. You curled in the dark, alone and in pain, hungry and hopeless. You thought about your fate and waited for death. Suddenly, the iron door opened and you saw the man who spat on you. He was a palace official, decked in ceremonial robes which he soon removed to show you his body.

'Spit on me.'

You glared at the sores covering his body. There was no clean patch of skin. After he removed his robes, all you could see were slime, pus, maggot, and blood in varying states of staleness. Even in the stinking prison cell, his own stench stood out.

'Spit on me!'

You were baffled, you thought this might be some fever dream that you hallucinated on the verge of death, but you had the presence of mind to request some water. You hardly had any saliva left to swallow, let alone to spit.

The palace official disappeared, and a platter of food arrived. You were presented with platefuls of delicious hot food, accompanied with jugs of cool sweet water. You were sure all the good stuff were packed with poison, but you didn't care. At least you would die with a full stomach.

It turned out that you did not die. You felt better and stronger. The good food kept coming, for what you presumed were dinner and breakfast. And soon after you ate your fill of the breakfast, the heavy cell door was pushed open again.

'Spit on me.' The official sounded almost like he was begging you.

It was extremely awkward, but you obliged. You spat all the saliva, mucus, and phlegm you could dredge up your throat, right onto the official's maggoty body. The whole experience felt surreal, and you were still mostly convinced that after all these theatrics, you were eventually going to die. Once you had exhausted your jaws and dried your mouth, the official put his robes back on and left without another word. You were in the dark about what was going on, but when the platters of food still arrived later for noon and evening meal, you were too happy to think too much.

After the evening meal was cleared, and you were patting your full tummy, the official appeared again. He looked definitely happier. He let you out, with several parting words.

'Go to your people. Tell them tomorrow, the Ruler and his entourage are coming to visit.'

Your story ended there, leaving your audience astonished.

'I can't believe it!'

'You're joking!'

'Are you sure you weren't just hit on the head by a fallen branch?'

For thirty years, nobody had walked out or been dragged out of the ghetto, and returned safely in one piece. Being fed good food and told to spit on an Empire official was also unthinkable.

'What was the offer? What is it going to be?'

'Why did you spit on him?'

'Why did he want you to spit on him?'

'Did you ever get to see the Ruler?'

'What food did they let you eat? Did they drug you and make you crazy?'

'Is this a trap to kill us all?'

You could not give a satisfying answer to any of the questions, so you merely shrugged, shook your head, and scratched your hairy armpits. Your excitement was gradually turning into apprehension, with a growing amount of fear.

'I don't know what this all means, either. All we can do is wait and see.'

The Ruler and his entourage arrived in a grand procession. Royal musicians played drums and trumpets, while members of the palace and military soldiers marched on their feet or rode mounts. You saw several animal-drawn carriages as well. The humble shacks in the ghetto seemed to be shaken by the sounds of their thumping feet and pounding drums.

'Hide the women and children. Prepare secret exits. At least some of them should be able to survive.' Earlier, you had told your folks to anticipate the worst. They may have fed you and let you out, but you knew that these people were cruel and unpredictable.

You and two other ghetto men approached the Ruler's entourage. Your heart was going to bound out of your chest. This was the Supreme Ruler, who had once ordered for your people to be killed and burned, and now he came in person to see the very people he had despised so much he called them untouchables. As expected, the Ruler remained on his mount. He refused to as much as set foot on the contaminated soil of the ghetto.

'Official. Show them what happened.'

The palace official who came to see you in the cell walked forward, and unclasped his belt. His ample body was exposed for display. There were folds of flab, thick fatty flesh, and rough hair unkempt . . . but no fresh sores. Only drying scabs, on good way to healing.

'Your sores . . . are healing!' You blubbered. You couldn't believe it. Not a single maggot in sight, nor any pus or slime.

'Your saliva was a cure.' The official admitted, with reluctance in his voice.

'A disgusting cure for a disgusting disease!' The Ruler snapped. Behind the iron mask covering his face, no doubt disfigured by the sore, you could see his bloodshot, red-rimmed eyes.

A tense silence ensued. Nobody was quite sure how to proceed next, but after a few moments, you ventured a question.

'What brings you here, Supreme Ruler?'

The Ruler did not deign to speak to you, but the chubby official answered. He was too happy to be cured, his attempts to show arrogance was only half-hearted.

'We need your spit. Spit from you, and from your people.'

'But we are untouchables. The Empire never recognized our existence. We are dirty, contaminated, and impure. We will infect anything that we touch.'

'Please, this epidemic has gone beyond control. Nothing we tried to do was successful. Our doctors, our medicinal herbs, our spells and tinctures . . . all failed. The only thing that has helped was your spit, and we were sure, the rest of your people has spit that can cure us too.'

You and your two friends remained silent. Anger simmered in your heart and started to boil. The years of discrimination and bullying wasn't going to be brushed aside easily.

'Please. This epidemic could bring the Empire to its knees. If the rebels and the Western Kingdom found out about this . . . there will be war. The Empire might fall.'

Not too bad, you thought. The Empire rising or falling was never much of your concern, and would bring no difference whatsoever to the living condition of your people. If anything, under a new rule, perhaps your people would be treated more kindly.

You glanced at the Ruler's eyes; they were brimming with disgust and hatred. You knew if you refused their request, they will forcefully make you do it. Better make the most of the occasion. You already had the next steps planned.

'We will spit you all to health, with three conditions.' You looked at your two friends, giving them the cue.

'First,' said your friend on the right, 'the ghetto-dwellers will no longer be discriminated against. Not anymore. We are going to live with the Empire citizens, out there in the open.' The Ruler snorted.

'Second,' your friend on the left continued. 'The ghetto-dwellers will be given houses and lands for us to work on. Anywhere we choose to build our new life.'

Tension hung in the air, as everybody waited for the final condition.

'Third.' Now it was your turn to speak. 'All the diseased Empire citizens must gather in the amphitheatre, while the ghetto dwellers will climb up the podium and spit on them from above. No one would be exempted, including the Ruler, the officials, and the advisors.'

When they dragged you to the city prison, you had seen the amphitheatre. You only remembered seeing it as a child, before the catastrophe happened. It used to be a symbol of unity and prosperity, where Empire citizens get together for important events, while the ghetto dwellers were never even allowed to see it. Now the structure will bear witness to the freedom of the ghetto-dwellers—freedom against oppressors from their own fellow citizens.

The Ruler's mount whinnied and lifted its two front legs, while the Ruler unsheathed his sword.

'Damn you, dirty, despicable people!'

The accompanying soldiers whipped out their weapons too. The tense silence shattered into pieces, sharp enough to wound.

You trembled at the impending disaster. Yet you stood your ground. With quivering voice, you told them,

'We were unarmed. We were poor people without means of defence. You could easily kill us all.' You gulped, swallowing your now precious saliva.

'But remember, dead people cannot spit.'

The chubby official whispered to the Ruler, and calmed him down. The impending doom seemed to dissipate into the afternoon air. After several orders barked by the Ruler, the whole entourage returned to the city.

You took several deep breaths, full of relief and gratefulness. History that once was erased, now was brought back to life, and would soon bring life to the Empire. Tomorrow you and the rest of the ghetto-dwellers will return to live and breathe among the civilized, like resurrected ghosts returning from the dead.

'Wait, I still don't get it. What turns our spit into cures?' The friend on your right asked, after the last of the Ruler's entourage has disappeared.

'I guess I don't know,' you shrugged. With a tiny smile, you looked out of the corner of your eyes at the tiny speck of chewed purplish-blue berry on your friend's chin.

After Time 12: The Flood

'Remind me a reason why do I trust you, o young man. I am not starting to doubt my own dreams now.'

You kept your head bowed in respect. The brain in the head was whirring urgently, arranging and rearranging the correct words to say.

'This is the largest gamble I am ever tempted to take. First, you requested five crates of Black Gold. That would be a huge chunk off the government's reserve, enough to support two seasons of scarcity. I am very, very concerned.'

The king of the Western Kingdom anxiously paced the small room. His tall, willowy figure was a stark contrast to your own shorter form, with the slightly hunched back.

'Second, you brought me here, the highest peak in the enemy territory. I am technically committing suicide, entering a lion's den unarmed. My presence here is under the strictest confidentiality, only known to you and my most trusted men. Great disaster will befall me and my kingdom if this ever leaks out.'

You nodded quietly in agreement. You knew the seriousness of this venture you were undertaking. The King wore a peasant robe made of coarse wool with raw cotton twisted into thick ropes for belt. His face was obscured with a hood, and he grew his face hair long like the common men in the area. Other than his uncommonly tall stature, the disguise was perfect. You had been extremely careful. Barring outright betrayal, you were sure that the secret would stay protected.

'Third, you made my men carry a boat to the top of a mountain, a real mountain with steep ridges, cliffs, and ravines! This is triple craziness!

Where are we going to sail? There is neither river nor ocean on this dastardly high and cold place! There is barely a stream flowing between cracks of rocks—ah, what tricks are up your sleeve, o young man?'

You remained silent, cautious. The King, despite his misgivings, had shown remarkable faith in your plans. You accepted that his suspicions were justified. You were foreign to him, and he, to you. The people of the Western Kingdom and the Empire of the East do not look alike, practice different cultures, and were essentially strangers to each other. The Westerners were fair and tall, with thick silvery-white hair. Meanwhile the Eastern people have coal-black hair, and mostly have shorter statures. Most importantly, the people of the East and the West were essentially enemies, rivals to each other.

There was no reason why their people should trust a stranger like you.

However, fate stated otherwise. Two months ago, the King himself visited you. You were with your family, together with the rest of the band of refugees hiding in a village deep in the inland valleys of the Western Kingdom. He said that a message in a dream guided him there.

'I saw you standing on the ruins of the post-historic empire, far in the east. You destroyed the enemies of my kingdom. I kept seeing the dream, over and over again. Is there any truth in what I saw?'

'I am a poor man with nothing in my possession. You could see for yourself, Great King.'

'My dream, it must have meant something.'

'Probably, Great King. I could try to interpret its meaning.'

'What do you mean, o young man? Can you read dreams?'

'I may be able to, Great King. It was an old profession, something my ancestors had done many years ago. I might have read something about it in the ancestral tomes.'

After that, it was not difficult to convince the King to follow your plans, although many times, even you were uncertain of what you said. In his excitement to defeat his Eastern enemies, the King was fixated on his dreams, and easily concurred with your interpretations. This long and bloodied strife between the *Homo sanguinis* had been going on for too long—two civilizations beyond their prime, going at each other's teeth and claws, while the body counts kept rising. Perhaps the opportunity to draw a clean ending to the saga has finally arrived.

Your ancestors came from the Empire of the East. The first people who built a new civilization after the history of the previous generation were buried under the rubbles of apocalypse. A long time ago, one of your ancestors had served the ruler of his time. Your grandparents told you about him, but the name had been lost when the story was passed down through the generations. He had been thrown to prison, and learnt how to read from a fellow prisoner. As soon as he was released from prison, your ancestor made his way to the Western Kingdom, together with several volumes of ancient history and prophecies of the future of the Empire. The books remained as secret family heirlooms, while back in the Empire, books were burnt and reading, outlawed.

'I trust you to carry out this task. Tell me anything that you may need. Together we must emerge triumphant.' That was the King's words to you, two months ago.

* * *

It was an extraordinary landscape.

The forest basin had been left undisturbed for decades, maybe centuries. The floor was covered with thick shrubbery and creeping undergrowth, while huge tree trunks soared to the sky. The trees may be around the age of the old dam nearby, probably older. An old fortress, long deserted, the walls broken into gaping holes and trailed with intertwining vines. Remnants of abandoned settlements could be seen scattered here and there, merging with the plant and animal life thriving after the humans had left. For many years, this patch of land had been untouched by civilization. No man-made noise or voice was heard here—except for the deafening rumble of water from the dam.

When the Sovereign Ruler and his entourage arrived, the basin was thronged with people. Noisy, without much sense of order. Most the thick undergrowth and bushes were already hacked off, drying leaves and broken sticks lying in piles. Once pristine and covered, now bare patches of earth lay exposed, alternately turned into muddy puddles during rainy days or crumbled into dust when the sun was scorching hot. Everyone brought their digging tools, barrows and bundles, tents and straw mats. Discovery of Black Gold in the area had become sensational news, spreading like wildfire all over the Empire.

'How did all these people find out? I have ordered that this be kept as royal secret!' The Ruler glared at all his courtiers and advisors. Each of them looked down, trying to avoid his angry gaze, none had any answers to give.

'Hey young man. Show me where you found the Black Gold.'

Obediently, you crawled ahead, going past the Ruler's mount, and the rest of his entourage. You headed to the direction of the dam, stopping at a thick clump of growth about ten arms' length from the brick walls. You made a gesture to the Ruler, indicating the spot.

'Here?' the Ruler stopped his mount. The rest of his courtiers and advisors also froze in their tracks, some jumping down before hurriedly trying to conceal their excitement.

'Set up camp here. I want the whole area to be fenced, cordoned off, from the walls of the dam, up to thirty arms' length inland. Only royal workers must be allowed to work here. Nobody else should be let in.'

The story that began to spread through the grapevine three days ago was this. You had stumbled upon a rough black lump, softer than stone but harder than clay, right there near the walls of the dam. It was as big as your own ankle. You didn't even know how important it was, until you blurted the story out to the people in the city you saw later, and they reminded you of the legends of the Black Gold. You were merely a farmer, crossing the woodlands as a shortcut to get to the city with your produce to sell. You were taking a breather on a tree stump, checking and sharpening your tools, when a glint in the soil caught your attention.

That was also the story that you told the Sovereign Ruler, and every person of the Empire who spoke to you.

The miraculous story of the Black Gold ore attracted people like moths to flame. Initially one or two people came, looking around, trying to ascertain what the rumour was all about. Then more people arrived. The people brought tools with them, and they started to dig. Bit by bit, the ground was explored, and finally, one of the dozens of hopeful diggers found another piece of Black Gold. Authentic black, dark and glistening gold. Dozens became hundreds; all of them were expectant of hoarding good fortune very soon.

What a blessing to the Empire. Who would have believed that for centuries they had been walking on treasure? Who would have known that chunks of Black Gold were lying quietly right under their feet, waiting to be discovered?

People came from all eight corners of the empire. North, south, east, west, and the points between. A small piece of Black Gold is enough to feed a family for years. Motivated by the promise of a better life, they came with hope and whatever effort each could muster. Old and young, women and children. They dug the earth and refilled the holes, and then they pushed their shovels and hoes at the same patches again, with undying hopes.

The common people's practice of treasure-seeking was already making an incredible scene in the area surrounding the old dam. When the royal gold diggers came and laid their stakes, the picture became even grander.

Fences were built, labelling the area as off-limits to anyone but the royal workers. Seven splendid tents were erected for the workers and supervising officials. Their duty was to find and gather Black Gold for the Sovereign Ruler. The Ruler had found out about the gold-mining frenzy, and he definitely wanted to win the race.

The civilian-seekers who had been exploring the area for almost three days were driven out and kept away by guarded fences. Anger boiled and exploded. Black gold was a gift from nature; it didn't solely belong to any particular person, not even the Ruler. The people demanded their fair share, and several young men were particularly persistent. A brief scuffle ensued which quickly ended in bloodshed. Two corpses, their chests drenched with blood after meeting the swords of the royal soldiers were heaved away and thrown into the river.

'The area we fenced off is put under the royal decree. I am not preventing you from seeking your own fortune. What I am requesting for is that you, my people, stay away from the royal grounds. Please mine for your share elsewhere.'

After being dismissed by the Ruler like that, the people had no choice but to obey. They did not have the power and weapons to fight. Nevertheless, their desire and greed for Black Gold remained just as strong. Outside the fenced grounds, the people kept digging, and their number continued to increase, despite the smaller area available for the crowds. Several times in the day at various spots amidst the crowd, the people broke into fights, most of the times shedding blood. The craze for Black Gold was infecting everyone.

The day turned into night, and when dawn broke the following morning, there was literally no stone left unturned. Every single patch of soil surrounding the dam had been already dug up.

The water in the dam kept rumbling, loud and deafening, above the din of the people.

* * *

'It will be a grand show, o Great King.'

'What do you mean?'

You stretched out your hand, pointing your finger to the south.

From the top of the mountain, the view was amazing. Vast area of the Empire's geography could be observed, including the Empire capital, the giant amphitheatre, and the great dam. The southern region had been thriving with development, as evidenced by the scattered grand houses, and bulky, towering stone buildings. The northern lands largely consisted of hills and mountain ranges, while the people lived off their farms, livestock, and forest produce. You could see wide patches of green, dotted by scattered human settlement. Meanwhile, a huge expanse of the ocean lay in the west, and beyond it, the land of the dreaded enemy, the Western Kingdom.

'I still do not get you.' The king of the Western Kingdom remained confused, but was patiently waiting for your explanation.

'According to the story that was passed down by my ancestors, the great dam was built about three, maybe four hundred years ago. The technology far exceeded its time, and was the brainchild of a young genius who eventually perished in jail, who was the victim of the ruler's paranoia.'

The King leaned his head a bit further to the direction you pointed, trying to ascertain the location of the structure.

'It was technologically advanced, but became isolated and forgotten, because nobody in the Empire inherited the knowledge to maintain it, let alone reconstruct a similar feat.'

'So, the dam has been neglected for hundreds of years?'

'Neglected. But behind the scenes, it has been empowering the Empire with progress for all those centuries!'

'How amazing! What a remarkable technology! And so unfortunately lost!'

'Yes, but everything is written in this volume.' You took out a book, hidden underneath the folds of your robe. 'This is one of our family treasures, written by the young genius.'

That took the King by surprise. His expression immediately changed.

'So, you do know the technology? You could replicate it?'

'No. It is too complicated, and I am not as bright as my ancestor.' You hid the volume back whence it came. 'But I do know how to defeat it. How to destroy it.'

After that, you kept your silence, giving the King time to think. It would be a major gamble for the Western Kingdom, putting great fiscal and potentially imperial stakes against tales inherited by a poor young farmer's family.

'What do I need to do now?'

'The wheels have been set in motion. As I have said earlier, Great King, it will be a grand show. Please sit back, relax, and watch as the show reveals itself.'

'Tell me more about this grand show. I cannot just sit and wait.'

'The time that we are living now, in this land and our land back home, is the post-historic time. The time, after time. Many more hundreds of years ago, humans have made great history. We were a globe-spanning, technologically advanced civilization which was erased by the greed for Black Gold and the evil in human hearts. After the dust has settled over the apocalypse, new civilizations rose, and we built a new history right over the ruins of the old. We are the *Homo civilis*. Unfortunately, history consists of repetitive clichés, following a simple formula each time. The only difference would be the people who act out the characters.'

'I know about the apocalypse in the past, and how the older generation has made mistakes. But I still do not see how that would relate to your plans. And what would we need to do with the boat that my men have painstakingly carried up this mountain?'

You admired the King's patience, in the face of his overwhelming curiosity. You knew he would be rewarded for it very soon. Deep in the southern region, the valley surrounding the dam was losing its green canopy. Reddish patches were appearing and expanding. The woodland was being chopped off, all the greens carved away to expose bare earth. Bare, naked earth with no more roots and shoots to keep the soil together.

About ten feet away from the dam, the Ruler was laughing heartily in his tent. He arranged pieces of Black Gold on a wooden table, forming columns, like marching soldiers. He spoke to an audience nobody else could see. Then he laughed again. Anyone walking outside and overhearing might have thought of his laughter as that of a madman. Underneath the table, more chunks of Black Gold were gathered in several small heaps.

Water in the dam kept rumbling, loud and deafening.

The grounds surrounding the dam were being turned inside out, the soil prodded full of holes. People were still digging, even deeper, with greater hopes and desperation. There was no sign of them ever slowing down.

Suddenly, the earth shook.

Starting with a hairline fissure, a crack in the wall extended rapidly, elongating on both ends. Hoes and spades hovered in the air, the diggers closest to the wall froze in their motions, their attention focused on the impending doom. Gradually as the others noticed what was going on, they too stopped. An ominous hush ascended over the valley.

Water spewed from the crack, in a small jet which grew bigger and stronger within seconds. The wall of the dam shattered into pieces, and a mountain of water roared behind it.

'Great King, the show has begun.'

You, the King, and everyone else on the mountaintop looked towards the south with amazement and terror. Massive waves of rolling water rushed inland, crushing against trees, hills, buildings, anything that stood in its path was reduced to floating rubbles. The roar of water drowned all other sounds—including the screaming humans.

'Is this all your doing, o young man?' The King spoke after a long-stunned silence. Far below, the terrifying sight continued to unfold.

'All I did was utilize their own greed against themselves. The five crates of Black Gold I requested were buried all around the dam. The dam is old and has seen zero maintenance over these centuries. Once the grounds that held its structure was weakened by mining works, the walls gave way all too easily.'

The water hit the mountain, and you could feel the shockwave vibrating to the top. The King's men hurriedly went to prepare the boat they had at the ready. You would need it to escape to the sea.

Nobody said anything. The King found neither voice nor words to say anything in the face of such astounding calamity.

The whole Empire was destroyed within moments. All evidence of its glory sank under the flood caused by the broken dam.

The moment of truth.

There was no need for anyone to write down the story because in no time, this history will repeat itself. *Homo historicus.*

Epilogue: The Land with no Sun

Dawn never broke in this land. For more than twenty years, the elders passed the tale to the younger generation. You were birthed from a dark world, to enter a dark world. The sun was only known to you by name, never by her light. Such wondrous tales were told of her—you listened with amazement, how she drew green shoots from the moist earth, called upon birds to leave their nests, and threaded rain down from the clouds. She bestowed glow upon the surface of lakes, and turned leaves into golden sheets. She tamed the edges of mountain rocks, and hardened the mud in paddy fields.

Ah! For twenty years your people learnt how to lead lives forsaken by the sun. This was indeed a cursed land.

'And suddenly you are telling me that the sun indeed exists? Are you crazy? You really deserve to be chained and forgotten in the darkest dungeons!'

'Chaining me in the darkness will not stop truth from coming to light.'

'What do you mean?'

The ensuing silence was only broken intermittently by the usual tortured gasp coming from the old man's direction.

The old prisoner was too strange, his marbles must have scattered too far for him to collect. Although you had never seen a face appearing from the dark behind the steel bars, you could imagine how he probably looked like. Scrawny and malnourished, with dirty tangled hair over his whole body and face. The stench of his unwashed body must be unbearable.

The sun died more than twenty years ago. The lore of your people said that a vengeful God doomed the humans to live in the dark. The earth was scorched by war. Smoke from the burning cities filled the sky and suffocated birds, while fish drowned in rivers congested with blood.

Before the grand-old war erupted, the earth was fertile, with orange-blue skies and yellow-green hills. No seed touched the soil without sprouting, no tree grew without bearing fruits. The people never fall sick, nor do they suffer from hunger. Conflicts rarely occurred, and even if they did, the scales were small, easily deescalated without casualties. This isolated land was the most blessed in this time after time.

The lore spoke of how this land was surrounded by seven greenish-blue hills, which were protected by an outer ring of seven brownish-yellow hills. Two rivers wound through the lush valleys, like two entwined dragons. Giant bananas grew in these valleys. You could take a bite of the milky white flesh and the rich taste stayed all day long. These bananas were huge, such that only one fruit would be enough to feed a small family for a day.

Blessings attracted envy. Warlords, pirates, and rulers of neighbouring lands stared at your land with greed, and soon their desire brought bloodshed. Barbaric armies appeared from between the hills, suddenly announcing,

'This land belongs to us, and these bananas are ours!'

The people of this land, led by their valiant Sovereign Ruler, took up arms against the barbarians. For thirty days they were killing and being killed. Like wildfire the battles spread across the land, destroying villages and farms, taking away limbs and lives. Rain and blood splashed onto soil, turning the living earth into putrid mud.

'Victory finally became ours. Victory rightfully belonged to the people of this land, and our valiant leader, the Sovereign Ruler. The Ruler led us to victory! He restored the honour of our land, protecting it from the filthy invaders!' You repeated the story, the way it was told over and over again in your land, by the old to the young, and by the young to each other.

The prisoner remained silent. His coughs sound harsher, more merciless, like his throat was grated with sandpaper.

'But the murders brought down God's wrath upon the people,' you continued, after waiting in vain for a response. 'The night after the war ended, they had a big celebration, feasting upon the bananas that they managed to defend. Then they all fell asleep with exhaustion. Alas! The dying embers of their bonfire was the last light they ever saw. When they woke up the next morning, the fire had died, and the night stayed. Dawn never breaks. The sun never comes. More than twenty years she has forsaken us. The Sovereign Ruler told us that we were doomed to live in the darkness forever, because of the curse brought by the barbarian armies.'

The prisoner still gave you no answer. His breath hitched more frequently and suddenly broke into what sounded like sobs.

He was weeping.

You were confused, but you kept your guard up. You knew you had already disobeyed the first rule as a prison guard: 'Never interact with a prisoner!' But curiosity had gotten the better of you. There was too much enigma in this prisoner to ignore. Wasn't he supposed to be someone feared by the whole nation? Even mentioning his name could make people's hairs stand on end.

You were born two years after the grand old war ended. The sun was already dead. The world was dark. Night and day were concepts not explained by light—instead like your peers, you made sense of the passage of time by sounds. There were birds and insects that were noisy at night and fell silent as day arrived, to be replaced by human sounds.

Since childhood you were taught to navigate your way in the dark. You felt your way around, sometimes a walking stick would be a useful guide. Your steps stumbled as you learn to move around obstacles you couldn't see. You smelled, touched, and listened—that was how your people evolved to survive, as your eyes were of no use. Eyes were nothing but two cursed orbs stuck in the skull, with no meaning other than tragedy.

You grew fit and well, trained by your family with the arts of war. Your body was sturdy, your reflexes quick. All of these you learnt without sight. Your nickname was the 'Seeing Warrior' because you seem totally unfettered by the dark. At a young age you were recruited as the Sovereign Ruler's elite guards, regarded as a prodigy, and finally you were tasked to guard an old dungeon, concealed in the deepest and long-abandoned pit in a corner of the Ruler's palace yards.

The people spoke of the mysterious dungeon in hushed tones, shivering at the unexplained horrors within it. They said that enchained in the cell was the most ferocious, beast-like prisoner, locked in there for decades. His strong body was twice the size of normal humans. He could break rocks and bend iron with his bare hands. Nobody dared to mention his name, let alone going to talk and listen to his voice. Stories of his notoriety spread across the land. Only the best guards were assigned to his cell, and today, that person was you. You were facing the feared monster.

The monster who was now weeping. Your ears will never lie.

'Which one was the truth? That there was no sun, or no people who saw the sun?' Once his sobs subsided, he began to speak again, inviting your curiosity.

'What do you mean?'

'You could not see the sun. Does it mean she was truly gone? Could she still be out there?'

'If she was there, where was her? What was she doing all this while?'

'She remained in her place, the glorious sun. She followed her routine, dancing across the sky from dawn to dusk, the way she has been since the beginning of life.'

'You're mad!' You yelled. 'You are not a dangerous criminal. You're nothing but a crazy old man!'

The prisoner retreated into his silence. He didn't have much energy to hold a conversation. His voice was feeble, and even breathing sounded like a chore.

'You were special, young guard. Come closer. I will impart to you, a truth.'

You inched nearer to the cell bars. Never in your wildest imaginations have you pictured yourself this close to the notorious criminal. Ah! Your curiosity was a horse straining against her reins.

'Tens of guards have appeared before my cell. They will come stumbling in the dark.' The prisoner paused, dragged a strangulated breath, and carried on.

'Every time they approached this cell, every single one of them would slip in the puddle in front of the main entrance. They would lose their footing, tripped, and fell before getting up and fumbling their way forward. All of them would fall, even the guards who were most familiar with the structures of this dungeon. There was only one exception. You.'

'How did that make me special?'

'You still didn't see it, did you? All the other guards, actually all the people of this land, were rendered blind after the grand war twenty years ago. All of them, except you. Truth is, the sun never dies. She never left. Instead, the sights of your people had died. Their eyes were forever closed to the light, and they believed that the world is nothing but darkness.'

'What madness are you spewing, old prisoner! If they are blind, and I am not, why did I never see the sun as well? I lived in the dark. Like you, like everyone else!'

'You were raised by blind people who did not know light. From the day you were born, they told you that the world was dark. They made you believe that the sun did not exist, even though you saw her every day above your head, burning your scalp with her penetrating warmth. A false reality was forced upon your mind, such that your eyes could no longer perceive the truth.'

His words were an arrow, straight to your heart. The shock stunned you. You could not formulate a reply, and let him carry on with his revelations.

'In the grand old war, all the people of this land were massacred by the barbarians, the pirates. They were slaughtered like animals. Their carcasses rotted without graves, piled on top of each other, swelling and bursting under the heat, lizards and scorpions crawling in the emptying skulls. Vultures and crows made this land their feeding grounds. No one survived.'

Now you were right in front of the iron bars, fascinated by this tale, so different from stories of the glorious past you used to know.

'Out there, the Sovereign Ruler, and the people who claim to be the sons of this land, were actually the invaders. Those robbers took possession of this land after massacring all the natives. And you, young guard, descended from them.'

'Wait, wait!' Your rage was provoked. 'The Sovereign Ruler was the hero who led the people to victory! You could tell so many lies and I may believe you, but do not insult the Ruler!'

'They told you that, didn't they? That was the falsehood they wanted the world to believe,' the prisoner's laughter reached your ears for the first time, and you noticed how frail it sounded. You didn't find anything funny in what he said. His pointless humour outraged you, triggered your impatience.

'Now did that have anything to do with the sun? With what you babbled about light and darkness? What about the wrath of God? Did God hide the sun, or did he make us blind?'

'You were right, young guard. My story has everything to do with the sun, light, darkness, and the wrath of God. This peaceful land hid a secret, only known to the natives. The giant bananas, growing wild in the valleys, coveted by many, actually harbour poison in their flesh.'

'Poison?'

'They were contaminated, from an even older war, a very long time ago. The poison made the bananas huge, many times the size of normal bananas. It was both a blessing and a curse—eating more than one banana a day, will render a human blind.'

'I . . . I never ate the bananas. My tongue will burn upon touching the sap. Since I was small, I learnt to avoid them.' As you spoke, you begun to realize something.

'Correct, young guard. That was why you were special. You were different from the others.'

You were at a loss for words, between amazement and disbelief. You rubbed your eyes. Wasn't this how darkness was supposed to look like? This was darkness, what you were seeing. You were birthed from the dark, to enter a dark world. No sun, no light, no sight. But was there really nothing to see?

'Old man,' your voice trembled. 'If you were telling me the truth, then tell me one more thing. How do I see the sun?'

This time, his silence dragged even longer. In the deafening quiet you could only hear the rise and fall of his chest, breath by strangled breath.

* * *

The cold morning felt sharp to your skin. You stood on a rock by the lakeside, your stance firm, facing the wind. Exactly following the old prisoner's instruction.

'There was no better place to find the sun. Every morning, the breeze blew inland from the east. The sun begins her ascent up the sky from that direction as well.'

The previous day's encounter with the old prisoner left an indelible mark in your mind. You kept recalling his stories, and his words of guidance.

'Close your eyes, tightly. Do not open them. Stand still, until your legs trembled with fatigue.'

How could the sun possibly be shining without anyone realising? You still find the whole proposition outrageous. Your younger days were filled with tales of her brightness. On days with the sun, her light would reach the tiniest crevices and the deepest of caverns. Rivers will display the secrets lying on their floors, while caves will open to show her their treasures. How was it possible that your people missed all of that, if the sun was really there all this while?

Half of your heart wanted to believe in the old man. Your nickname, 'The Seeing Warrior' must have meant something. You knew how miraculous your achievements were. You never missed a target with your bow and arrows. Your swords hit the mark all the time. Stumbling on your steps was unheard of. Most other warriors were able to navigate with their senses despite the perpetual darkness, but they still miss targets and stumble. You never did. Probably it was true. You were special, and the old man has revealed an important secret.

Nevertheless, the other half of your heart was doubtful. The old prisoner was most likely a madman, his sanity chewed and spat out by twenty years of solitude in the dungeon. Or he could have been a scheming trickster—attempting to trap you into distrust and treachery towards the Sovereign Ruler. His feeble voice may be a façade for malice. You tried to tell yourself to remain steadfast. This experiment was only to prove him wrong.

'Stand still, until your legs began to tremble with fatigue.'

Warmth gradually enveloped your whole body. Your legs trembled harder and harder, making it more difficult to maintain your position, and your eyes suddenly snapped open, overwhelmed by an intense burning sensation. It was exactly as the old man had predicted.

'A seeing person will feel the sting of sunburn. No seeing eyes can bear to meet her glare. If you were truly blind, you are not going to notice a thing, except tired legs.'

You fell on your knees, shielding your painful eyes with your hands.

The sun has glared upon you, and you, a mere mortal, could not bring your eyes to perceive her being. But now you knew that she was there, has always been there. The veil has been lifted. The old man was neither a madman nor a trickster.

Who was he, and why was he in prison?

The sun paraded her glory, bathing every leaf, rock, and tree with her light. The lake glimmered with a glow you have always seen, but only now realized. For twenty years you have been told lies! You believed that the world was dark, while in truth you were not taught to recognize light!

'Once your eyes were opened, you must leave this land. The price of this truth is your life. Walk against the direction of sunrise, towards a peaceful nation. Run away from the Ruler and his people. They are all blind. You can escape from them.'

You had not believed that they will amount to anything, but you still remember every word the prisoner said.

'They will kill you, or throw you in the dungeon to rot, if they knew you could see.'

You turned your head to the left. That was the western sky, where the sun will set. The old man told you to journey that way.

You turned your head to the right. You could see several tall structures from afar, and you knew those must be the towers of the Ruler's palace. Somewhere underneath the stone walls was the underground prison where the old man who opened your eyes was chained.

You stood up, and headed to your chosen direction.

Towards the Sovereign Ruler's palace, armed with a new truth

—The sun has never forsaken this land!